Kinda

spiritual

A CULTIVATED COLLECTION
OF THE NOT-SO-ZEN THINGS I THINK

KEVIN DAVI

Kinda

spiritual

A CULTIVATED COLLECTION OF THE NOT-SO-ZEN THINGS I THINK

KEVIN DAVI

Kinda Spiritual

ISBN 978-1-7359974-6-9

 *Veronica Lane Books*
Books That Make a Difference!

2554 Lincoln Blvd. Suite 142, Los Angeles, CA 90291 USA
Tel: +1(833) VLBOOKS +1(833-852-6657)
www.veronicalanebooks.com

Publisher contact:
etan@veronicalanebooks.com

DEDICATION

For Mom, Dad and Ali.
All the good that exists in these pages, comes
from a townhouse on Alcott Street.

The rest I must have picked up when you guys
weren't looking.

CONTENTS

Chapter 1

THROW THIS BOOK AWAY

In any type of speaking engagement, you should make sure that you know your audience. It doesn't do you a lick of good to have a fantastic speech written in English only to have a Spanish-speaking crowd in front of you. I've found the same thing goes for spirituality. I have groups of friends who have taken the dive into this realm, and I know that I can speak openly about chakras and energy and all the other 'woo woo' mysticism that seems to be popular in Southern California. I also have groups of friends back on the East coast that check out the minute I use a new age term. And that's fine. I don't blame them. I'm the kid they remember knocking himself out by running into a tree at Carlton Park when he tried to catch a pass. Not exactly your pinnacle of enlightenment. So when I speak to them about any type of religion or spirituality, I tread lightly. I've got to spin the words and speak their language with the intention of getting the same point across.

But you?

I have no idea who you are.

I have no idea why you would buy this book.

And right here right now, I want to give you the opportunity to throw it away.

It's not because I don't think I have anything useful or worth saying. I mean, if I didn't I probably wouldn't sit down and put pen to paper for so many months trying to make sense of all this. It's more because I'm not really sure this book is exactly what you're looking for.

I grew up in Staten Island, New York. Spent my formative years in this suburb of New York City playing sports and being raised in a Roman Catholic family. I had great parents and still do. They worked their asses off to send my sister and I to private school and have since done everything they could to support us in every endeavor we take on.

I went to college in Boston where I studied physical therapy in a condensed program that I was in for no real other reason than my parents nudging. It was a degree that guaranteed a job following graduation, but I really didn't give it any more thought than that. In college, I found meditation and pretty much bailed on Catholicism entirely in favor of weird Eastern and Shamanic approaches to the Spirit that forced me into mental gymnastics that the Catholic Church never could.

When I graduated, I set out west to see what life was all about. After a year in Phoenix, I landed in Los Angeles where I found yoga, reiki, hippies, festivals and a slew of other things that seemed to open up my mind to infinite possibilities.

Obviously, that's the short version, but if you read that for your cliff notes, I think you'd at least be able to pass a multiple-choice exam. Maybe if there was an essay, you'd struggle a bit, but just toss in whatever you think the bearded yoga instructor running around Venice is thinking about, and you might be right. But I really haven't had that big trial or tribulation. Nothing so astounding has happened to me that I feel like people really need to know the epic tale of my coming to the light. There are a million people on this planet that are fantastic teachers studying traditions passed down for years, and I haven't trained under any of them. The closest thing I've had to a teacher is a guy by the name of Brad Warner who writes books about Zen, and if you've read any of his work, there's a real strong possibility that you might consider this piece a cheap knock-off. Apologies to Brad for stealing and botching any ideas I may have learned from you. I've taken classes from some really special yoga teachers, even committed to a few on a regular basis, but even there, I wouldn't say I've really had a 'teacher' in the most accurate sense of the term.

Every time that I get close to a place where I feel like it may help me to commit to one path, I get a little gun shy. Catholicism sets you up with a healthy distrust for authority, but we'll get to that later. I once went to the SGI Buddhist temple in Santa Monica and had a really great experience chanting the lotus sutra. Being in one room with a ton of people, all creating the same vibration, left me feeling really good. But no sooner had I stepped out of their sacred space than they were trying to sign me up as a member of their sect. It all seemed pretty dirty.

So I haven't really chosen one path on my spiritual quest, if you can call it that. And because of my lack of commitment, I haven't been able to perfect one approach. Instead, I've gotten by on a pinch of this and a dash of that, taking the ideas that I like from books and teachers and throwing away everything that I don't.

In Kevin Smith's cult classic 'Dogma,' there is a scene where Chris Rock, portraying the thirteenth apostle, describes how Jesus is now in heaven pissed off at the human race for organizing religions behind him. JC, as he familiarly refers to the savior, says that mankind got it all wrong by taking a good idea and making a belief structure out of it. He then goes onto explain how the gap between an idea and a belief is about as wide as the Grand Canyon because you can change an idea when you're given new information. But a belief is different. A belief runs deeper.

I am deathly afraid of believing in something. Anything really. Because it is so incredibly possible that I am simply just one hundred percent wrong. The more I become convinced that what I am doing is right, the more damage I could be doing if I'm not.

Hitler. Manson. And more recently, Bikram. None of these guys were as simple as the early James Bond villain sitting in their evil lair plotting death and destruction for everyone. These are people that started with what they thought was a good idea. They took the idea and preached it so regularly that it then became their belief. They then took their belief and devastated the lives of others. Because they "knew they were right." Because they knew that they could change the world for the better. And as people came up to defy them, they saw themselves as heroes fighting for a worthy cause.

Now there's a lot of this shit where I live in LA. There are a lot of spiritual leaders and yoga masters, and meditation gurus that have done quite a bit of work on themselves. To hear their stories is to realize that these people have lived incredible lives and overcome obstacles that I can barely believe. And they came out the other side on top.

But the problem is that when you slay the dragon, you become the dragon slayer. You believe in your own hype, and you stare at other people in disbelief at the challenges that they can't, or simply won't, stand up to.

You've walked through fire, so why can't they? You've found the perfect method to combating life's struggles, and if they would only just listen to you then they could do the same. If they would only follow your way.

But I don't think there is any one singular way. I think a lot of what I say in this book, you'll disagree with. I think a lot of what has worked for me in the past, wouldn't work for me anymore and probably wouldn't have worked for you in the first place. We're different. And that's fine. If there were one book that was completely 100% right, then I think we would have found it by now, and we'd all be singing *Kumbaya* around the fire.

So this book isn't about being right, and it's not about walking the perfect path. It's not about spiritual enlightenment, and it's certainly not about being a saint. It's just about some dude. Some dude who grew up feeling like there was something more than could be explained by science, but didn't buy into what his early religious doctrines were telling him. It's a book that will hopefully show you the difference between knowing the right thing and doing the thing. In this book I'll try to share with you the struggles I have on walking a better path, and a few of the successes that I've had along the way.

So before we continue, I want to give you one more chance to take the advice of this chapter and throw this book away, because in these pages, there is no enlightenment to be found. There are only more challenges. But if you're not trying to be the next Gandhi and you're more concerned with playing your little part in something bigger, then why not give it a read. I promise not to sign you up for anything at the end.

Chapter 2

A HEALTHY DISTRUST OF AUTHORITY

Standup comedian John Mulaney has a joke about Catholicism where he compares it to playing trombone. Playing the trombone is something that we all dropped right after high school. Nobody is still playing the trombone. The millennial generation has disposed of their Catholic faith in a similar fashion. It's not really hard to see why. For all the good that the Catholic Church has done, there have been some unthinkable crimes that have been committed. From the molestation of little boys to the crusades and inquisition, the track record does not leave you thinking of the word 'infallible.'

I grew up in a Catholic school. From preschool through eighth grade, I attended Our Lady Star of the Sea. If I hadn't been placed into one of three specialized public high schools in the city, I most likely would've ended up at either Monsignor Farrell's all boys Catholic High school or St. Joseph's by the Sea for another four years. You can guess which one I preferred.

Growing up, my friends around the neighborhood got to go to school wearing whatever they wanted. I would suit up in a polo shirt and slacks. Church on Sunday was a regular. In 6th grade my parents made me learn how to be an altar server like my older sister, they figured it would at least give me something to do at mass. It actually wasn't all that bad. We had half days every Wednesday and had days off for some nondescript holidays like the Assumption and the Ascension, although more than that, I remember not being off from school for the Jewish holidays like the kids on my block.

I'm actually incredibly grateful for my parents sending me to Catholic school early on. In the nineties, Catholicism had lost a lot of its fire and brimstone. Gone were the days that my dad had told me about where a six- foot-five nun would whack him in the back of the head or rap his knuckles with a ruler. If there was anything inappropriate going on, I was never aware of it. Our only nun was a cute little old lady who was going senile at a rather rapid rate. I remember being a bit scared of her in the way young kids are afraid of old people for no other reason than that they look really, really old. She would come to class once a week to collect money for the missions. My one piece of religious advice that I remember receiving from her was a very strong appreciation for The Virgin Mother. Even as young children, she encouraged us to pray to Mary. She told us that in the same way we loved our mothers, Jesus so loved his. So if she asked him to do something, he would want to make her happy, and it would probably get done. As a little kid, that really connects with you.

We also had a number of priests during my time in school that had positive impacts on me. Father Angelo's filler phrase during his homily was always, "and so my dear friends." My dad and I always hoped for Father Bob at Church because he had the best homilies. Father Eric got there a little later --when I was closer to sixth grade -- but he had a really simple way of talking to a young adult that made you feel like he wasn't patronizing you. A rare but important talent.

Then there was Monsignor Jeff. I never really understood what a Monsignor was, but it seems to be a particularly honored priest. Monsignor Jeff was head of our parish. He was a recovering alcoholic who often worked those struggles into his sermons. As an altar server, we used grape juice for the blood of Christ rather than the traditional red wine. He was one of the biggest Yankee fans I've ever met and even organized our eighth grade trip to

Camden Yards to see the Yankees play the Orioles. He coached the boy's baseball team for a while, though I never got to play for him. He knew every kid in the school by name. Even at a young age, you could tell that this was a man who cared about his flock.

Yet with all of these great role models within the Church, I chose to stray from the path that had been laid out in front of me before I could even fully understand it. Let's explore why.

I remember a sermon that Father Bob told at Sunday Mass once. He told the story of a little boy who wanted to know what happened when he died. He first approached his mother with the question. She told him that when you die, you go into a peaceful sleep forever. That didn't work for this little boy. He didn't want to sleep forever. So he went to his priest and asked what would happen to him when he died. His priest told him that he would go up to heaven where he would live with God and all his angels for all of eternity. The boy wanted to know what he would do in heaven. The priest told him that he could spend all of eternity looking at God's kneecap, and he would never be bored of it. This, of course, didn't work for the little boy either. Because how interesting is a knee cap? The boy wandered around thinking about the answers he had been given when he stumbled upon a dead bird. Being a curious little boy, he picked up the bird and began to examine its feathers. He was struck by the beautiful intricacies of each individual feather on the bird. In that moment, the boy realized that if God had put so much work into the feathers of a small bird and was said to love him infinitely more than the bird, he had nothing to worry about. God would see him through and take care of him in all things.

I was on board with this story for a while. And yet, heaven made no sense to me as a small child. When you think about it, death makes no sense to you as a little kid, but really heaven made it even more difficult to understand. The mom's answer was practically useless at the time. The idea of non-existence is just simply incomprehensible. Then the priest explains that you'll always be happy and content. Little kids get bored in five minutes, so that was another no-go for me. I could really understand the frustration of the child in the story. I could feel that disbelief in what the adults around him were saying. But the bird just circles you back to accepting that everything is going to be great without understanding how it's going to be great. I remember another time where one of our priests was telling us that in heaven, you could play baseball with Babe Ruth if you wanted to. Sports was a language that I could understand, but that definitely seemed like bullshit. I was a gifted young athlete and didn't want kids who couldn't play to be in the games that I was in. So if heaven was a game where everybody wins, or we don't keep score, I just didn't want it.

I was inquisitive about all of this. And let's take a moment to defend the adults around me because nobody really has an answer for these existential questions. You may have ideas without any concrete evidence to prove one thing or another. Yet, I kept getting answers. When you know that a question is a difficult one and someone gives you a quick and definitive answer, you're inclined to disbelieve it.

More so than the actual religious institution that was my church, I became increasingly frustrated with the school that it was attached to.

Our Lady Star of the Sea taught preschool through eighth grade. Each grade was broken up into two classes. So in second grade, you were either in class 2-1 or 2-2. Up until fourth grade, you had one teacher who would teach you all of the subjects.

Once you got into fifth grade, teachers would switch classrooms to teach different subjects. For a kid obsessed with moving around and activity, it was an absolute nightmare to sit at one desk for the entirety of the day. On top of that, if a good friend of yours wasn't in your class, you basically didn't see them for the year. Every adolescent felt that the system was unfair, but this setup may have left me a little bit more salty than I could have been.

I hated school. My mom says that when she first started bringing me to preschool some of the other kids would get there early to play outside before the doors opened up. But not me. My Mom would time it perfectly so that she could drop me off just as the doors were opening up.

"Mommy, I'm not going to school today."

"Okay Kev."

This was our dialogue on the way to school. But one way or another, she got me to go. And I sat in classes bored out of my mind. School came very easily to me, but the same could not be said of my classmates. With only two classes to choose from, it wasn't like the public school system where they could fast-track some of the smarter kids. No, we moved at a snail's pace for every student to grasp the material. I remember the kids who really pissed me off because they just couldn't get it. Looking back, I don't really have a problem with that. Every kid needs the opportunity to learn. But I remember getting in trouble at school for the most inane things. An untucked shirt,long hair, pants that were not the exact make of the pants that the school had issued. My grades were impeccable and yet, the focus was on all this other shit that in my mind shouldn't have mattered.

The biggest crime of all came in sixth, seventh and eighth grade where the math teacher was, and I say this with no reservations whatsoever, a raging bitch. Math has been my strongest subject. It just made sense to me. Every teacher that I had up until that point was perfectly content with how I went about my business because I understood the work. This teacher had issues with the way that I did my work. Every answer would be correct, and I'd lose points for how I arrived at my own conclusion.

She insisted that I show the work for my problems. So I dug my feet into the ground and refused to show any work for anything. While explaining problems in class, I would stare off out the window, looking bored as anybody. She'd single me out to answer a question that she thought I hadn't been paying attention to, but I'd answer without even switching up my gaze.

OK granted, I was a bit of a punk.

But that's just it. Everything seemed off growing up in that environment. The little things were made to be very important, while what I figured was the big picture was downplayed. I was expected to take the word of my priests and teachers as right, but I could see just in the way that I solved math problems that it didn't have to be their way. There wasn't one way to do it. There were several ways.

Fast forward through some very adolescent Holden Caulfield type years, and you'd find me bumming around guided meditation classes in college. I was looking into different cultures and religions and just kept coming up short. The names of God and the sacraments and holy days seemed to change, but the core belief structures were always there. Believe. Have Faith.

I used to pray for faith. Honestly, I wanted to know what it felt like to know, to really know that God held you in the palm of his hand because hard as I tried it just didn't seem real to me. None of the other choices seemed real either.

And then I stumbled upon a book. I don't know how I found it. Don't know who may have recommended it or where it came from, but I know that it was an important moment in my life.

The book was called *Hardcore Zen* by Brad Warner. I'll save you my fanboy fawnings over this masterpiece and get straight to the point that hit me right in the feels. In Brad's book, he encouraged you to question everything. Ironically when I would meet him years later and ask him to go deeper into this thought, he admitted that he was a little upset with his editor for making that such a big part of the book. But that's neither here nor there because in this instance, it's not necessarily what he meant, but how I took it. For someone who had grown up with priests in front of him telling me to believe, believe, believe! This was the first time in my life that a spiritual teacher had invited me to question. He wanted me to try some of the things that he offered, but at the same time dispel this notion that he had figured something out so perfectly that he now had all the answers. His practice of Zen was something that had helped him immensely, but he offered none of that to you. He simply said that you would have to try it for yourself and see.

That's where my faith, or lack thereof, stands today. I have not been able to commit to any one religious sect, though many have tried. My main reasoning for this is that I don't want to be locked in. Perhaps Kevin Smith was right when he created

Dogma. Maybe Jesus would be angry if he was where the world was today. Maybe he would have had a problem with organized religions and creating belief structures because beliefs are so hard to change. It's so difficult to take something that you have faith in and have attached yourself to, then turn around and question it.

And yet, those are the things that are probably the most important to question!

The Catholic Church's Nicene Creed has changed over the years, but while I was there, the beginning went something like this:

We believe in one God,
Father Almighty Creator of Heaven and Earth
of all that is seen and unseen.

Blind faith. That is what these opening lines are asking for. And it's something that I could never get behind. A lot of terrible things in this world have been made possible by blind faith, and I want no part of it. I want to continue to question, explore and see for myself. If you do too, then let's keep going

Chapter 3

MY PARENTAL COMPLEX

It probably will not surprise you that I have spent time in and out of therapy. The wheels in my brain never stop turning. I overthink and overanalyze everything that comes my way, try as I might to portray the super Zen go-with-the-flow type dude. An ex-girlfriend once accused me of being a closet control freak. I'm not going to say she was right. It's way too early in this book to give anybody that type of satisfaction. But I will cop to my own neuroses. And therapy, during the times that I've committed to it, has been helpful in working out some of my own shit.

One therapist that I worked with had what I found to be a very interesting take on why I moved out to the west coast. You see, I grew up with a certain success about me. Always did well in school. Always excelled at sports. On my dad's side of the family, I was the oldest grandson to the oldest son and emphatically my grandmother's favorite. On my mom's side, I wasn't quite the oldest, but I was showing a bit more promise as far as an Irish ex-NYPD sergeant was concerned. One of my uncles referred to my mom, dad, sister, and I as the All-American family. If you drew it up for a sitcom, it really wouldn't be far from the truth.

My parents live about a 5-10 minute walk from one set of grandparents and a 15-minute drive (without traffic) from my other grandfather. My dad stops in to say hi to his parents almost every week. My mom stops by to drop off meals and check her father's vitals every week without fail. They've both taken up the responsibility to look after their parents. They both operate in realms that I'm sure make their parents nothing but proud of them.

My therapist suggested that I didn't want that for myself. She suggested that my move to the west coast was an attempt to ditch out on some of the responsibilities and expectations that may have been placed on me had I stayed on the east coast in New York or Boston. I initially told myself that I would leave New York for five years before coming back so that I could learn something.

I would become a good physical therapist and get through some of the growing pains in other communities so that when I came back home, I would be worthy of the good name that my parents had created for themselves.

But maybe I wanted to create my own name.

A recurring character in any epic adventure is the orphan who becomes a hero. Jon Snow from *A Song of Ice and Fire* is a bastard with no claim to the family he grows up with. Luke Skywalker is raised by his aunt and uncle on a moisture farm he feels no connection to. Aladdin is a street rat orphan who is all alone in the world except for Abu. And all of these characters wind up going on epic adventures that captivate our imagination and prove the true spirit and resilience of the human condition.

So why is it so important that these characters start off their journey without a traditional parental figurehead to guide them?

It's to keep the altruistic aura of the hero intact. Think about it. Jon Snow over and over and over again tries to do the right thing. He dedicates his life to The Watch; he defends his brother and accepts every insult thrown his way at Castle Black, all in the name of doing the right thing. But there's somebody who sees through all this mess. Somebody, he can't bullshit. And that somebody is Mance Rayder of *Game of Thrones*.

When he first meets the King Beyond the Wall, he tries to lie and say that he wishes to join the free folk because his heart yearns to be free. Mance sees through this.

"No, Jon Snow," he says, "What you want to be, is a hero."

There it is. Jon Snow wants to be a hero. From his earliest days growing up in Winterfell, he was made aware of his place as the bastard. He could not inherit. He could never be Lord of Winterfell. So he wanted something else. He wanted a way to prove his worth. In other words, his ambition is a selfish one.

Even though his acts are selfless, it all begins as a way to make a name for himself. Now, as someone alone in the world, we can't really do anything but support him in making his own way. No one else helped him along in the way that a parent would, so he is untethered by that love and connection. Even when he tries to defect in order to join his brother's army and avenge Lord Eddard Stark's death, we are inclined to root for him to return to The Watch rather than defend his family.

And I think it's because we don't really recognize that family as his. His real family is not one of blood, but it's one that he created.

One thing that you have to understand about me is that I have the two greatest parents of all time. I can honestly say that there is not a thing that I wish they had done differently with me while I was growing up. My parents encouraged me to play sports and then drove me to each and every game and practice I had on the schedule. I actually thought it was weird that my cousins only played one sport per season. My mom pushed me to do well in school when all I was interested in was playing ball, and my dad supported her by threatening to take those teams away from me if I didn't shape up. We didn't have all the money in the world, but my parents worked incredibly hard and provided my sister and I with vacations and opportunities and everything else that's part of this great American dream.

So with this great childhood that I had, what the fuck am I doing in therapy? The truth is that I don't know. By all the standards and all the baby books, I guess I should've just kept on my path as the golden boy and be all set by now with a nice big house and a white picket fence. But I've still got my own problems. I still struggle with all the existential crises and day-to-day ups and downs.

That's why I've struggled at times with people who have a more interesting story than I do. When I say more interesting, what I mean is that there was a defining conflict. There was something to overcome. Divorced parents. Not enough attention. Moving from state to state. All those things that when we look back and do our own inner work, we can say, yup, that's the reason why I am the way that I am. I mean, in their case, it definitely makes sense. But in my case, I don't think it does. And I'd like to acknowledge my privilege here for a moment. I'm literally someone who had two loving parents and fantastic home life and upbringing, saying that maybe people who were not blessed with those privileges should stop whining about not having them. That's not really fair, and I can see how it would rub people the wrong way.

But think about all those celebrities that have everything—the house in Malibu, the fast car, the model partner. More money than they could spend in a dozen lifetimes. And they fly in and out of rehab like they're running a deal there.

These are the things that we dream about thinking, wow if I could just get this one thing, then I'd be really happy. And then they got all of it. Still nothing. Still problems.

Dave Chappelle, who I hope will be remembered as a great mind and hero of our time, put it best when he brought up Anthony Bourdain. He said, to the effect, this guy's job was to literally travel around the world eating the best food there is, and he killed himself! If that doesn't show you that happiness comes from within, then I don't know what will.

Because each opportunity that you are given is a double-sided coin. There are always positives. There are always negatives. It's probably the Libra in me talking, but I've always been able to see reasons for turning left and reasons for turning right, and for that matter, the reasons not to. Let's return to my parents.

I lived with my parents until I was 17 and I went off to college in Boston. My parents couldn't pay for all of my education, but they helped me where they could. I had a couple of scholarships to help and, for the rest, I took on some loans. I spent six years living in Boston, traveling to and from New York on the Fung Wah Bus for holidays and long weekends. If you're not familiar, the

Fung Wah bus (more affectionately known as the "China Bus") was a bus company that would take you from Chinatown in New York to Chinatown in Boston for less than $15. Buses left every half hour. In Boston, you would leave out of South Station, so it was pretty legit. But in Manhattan, there was just a little stand at the corner of Canal and Bowery where you'd buy your ticket, and then they would line you up on a city block. These buses absolutely *flew* up and down the east coast. We'd stop once at a rest stop for McDonald's and bathroom breaks, but I never once saw them fill up the tank. And once you got to your destination and got off the bus, they would be filling it up with new passengers right away. I have no idea how the whole system worked. Last I checked, these buses are no longer in service. Safety violations. Who would have guessed?

Anyways, when I spent my first year in Boston, I would come home every chance I got. Long weekends, short weekends, holidays—you name it. I'd always hop on the bus and make it back home to see my folks. But as I got older, the trips became a little less frequent. I started using Memorial and Columbus Day weekends to head north into Maine or to my friend's place in the Massachusetts boonies. I didn't need to go home as much.

For six years, it played out like that, and as I neared the end of my time in school, I had to think about where I wanted to live. It sure as shit wasn't going to be Boston. I love that city, I really do, but the winters are brutal, and I couldn't do another one. I had resumes out in California, Arizona, and I was lightly looking into a couple spots in New York.

The National Board of Physical Therapy is a bit mismanaged in that they only offer the licensing exam four times per year. You cannot register for this exam until after you have officially graduated from your university. And our graduation was right after the cut-off for the next exam registration. So basically you graduate and then have three months where you can't work as a physical therapist because you're not licensed. Stupid shit, really. But my parents were cool enough to let me stay in their house rent-free for three

27

months while I studied for my exam. I hadn't lived with my parents for a while at that point. I did some six-month stints while working internships in Manhattan at their house, but I had so much work and such a long commute that it really didn't even feel like I was there that often.

The three months prior to my exam were different. I literally didn't have a job. I would wake up, eat breakfast, and study. Then I would go to the gym, eat lunch, and study. Then I would go for a run, eat dinner, and study. I was in the house constantly. My old friends from high school had already started professional careers or were no longer living on the island. Everyone was busy, so it was really just me occupying my time. And again, I want to point out how great my parents were. In these three months, I didn't pay rent, or for food, and for the most part, they left me to my business. These relationships are always difficult as the dynamic changes when we get older. You're no longer their sweet baby boy, but really you'll always be their sweet baby boy. So tensions can ride high. But ours never really did (as far as I know. You may have to reach out to Lorraine for her side of the story.) We all went about our business and played our roles well. Played our roles.

My role was the good son. Who had been taught well, given opportunities, and was making the most of them. In all of my childhood and adolescence, there was really only ever one big fuck up. That's all. But that one big fuck up was something that really weighed on me.

After prom in high school, all the kids from my school went down to Wildwood, New Jersey for the weekend. It's a regular thing Staten Island kids do where you get a motel that turns their head the other way as you drink and smoke and whatever else while on their grounds. Well, one night, I decided to take my party elsewhere. More specifically, to the beach. Where you are not supposed to be after dark. And where you are definitely not supposed to be drinking underage. And where you are really really not supposed to be smoking substances that are illegal in the great state of New Jersey Yeah, this was a fuck-up on my part.

So I got myself arrested. Nothing really happened, though. I was 17, so the charges got expunged like a month or two later. But my dad had to come to pick me up, and he was pretty pissed. We didn't talk for a couple of days. I knew I had disappointed him. We actually had to drive down to Wildwood again later in the summer for a meeting with a mediator. Basically, since I was 17, I couldn't see a judge, so you meet a go-between and they decide what they are going to do with you. The whole meeting was pretty stupid. More white privilege stuff where because of my grades and my clean record and my going to college, they decided it wasn't a big deal and basically did nothing with it.

Then on the ride back to Staten Island, my dad did the best piece of parenting in his career. I remember what he said perfectly.

"Listen. I could ruin your summer right now. I could keep you from going to all of the graduation parties you had planned and lock you up in the house until you go away to school. But you turn 18 in a couple of months. And then you're an adult. And I don't agree with you smoking pot, but that's a decision that you're going to have to make for yourself going forward because they are your decisions going forward. But remember that you didn't get arrested for smoking pot. You got arrested for being a jackass. You were on a closed beach after dark that they patrol, smoking an illegal substance. That's just dumb. So make decisions for yourself but don't be stupid about it." And that was that. No further punishment. Just recognition of me as an adult. He knew he had taught me the best that he could, and now I was about to leave the nest, so to speak, and would have to figure it out for myself.

But I guess you could say that I felt torn by the whole situation. I was certainly sad that I had disappointed my father. That didn't feel good, and it wasn't a feeling that I wanted to get too familiar with. But I also disagreed with him. At that point in my life, I had been smoking pot pretty regularly for almost three years. I honestly preferred it to alcohol, and besides making a dent in my pocket and stupid movies funny, I didn't see any problem with the herb at all. He acknowledged he was more disappointed in the boneheaded decisions that got me into trouble with the law. But it wasn't his way. It wasn't something that he did. It wasn't something that he thought good and upstanding people did.

But here I was doing it. And it had brought me some of the most fun nights of my life. It had introduced me to some of the most interesting people of my youth. It had opened doors for me that would have remained closed for years to come if I had followed the D.A.R.E. way and just said no to drugs. So I wasn't really sure if his way was my way.

That may be why I live out on the West Coast.

I still love my family very much. I talk to my Dad weekly, and he's my most trusted business advisor. I text with my Mom weekly because I think we annoy each other on the phone at times, but it's all always love, and we are always checking in. But there are paths that I've taken and decisions that I've made that I know my parents disagree with. We'll get into a few of those in later chapters. And I've had an interesting time while on those paths considering what my mom or dad would think if they could see me here and now. Practicing a different form of religion. Taking drugs. Searching for truth. It's difficult to explain to them that I respect everything that they did, but I also have to find my own way. Every time I try to put it into words, it all comes out wrong.

And I consider some friends that I've made out here along the way. Crazy hippies that live in vans, *wooks* that take acid five times per week. Some intrepid travelers that have spent years studying in Bali. I think of the freedom that they have to do that and not always, but sometimes I notice that they don't feel as connected to their bloodline family. They feel more connected to their chosen family. Their chosen tribe.

And it's a beautiful thing. I don't have that same freedom. I'm trying to play with the balance because I will always be Tommy and Lorraine's boy, but there are times where all they'll be able to do is shake their head and hopefully smile. Because they taught me well, but now I'm out here in the field testing my knowledge.

Chapter 4

THE GREAT SCHISMS AND THE EGO

One of my more recent tattoos is an intricate black mandala on the back of my left hand. It took me a long time to get any tattoos that would be visible outside of a t-shirt and then even longer to commit to something on my hand, even though I've wanted something there for as long as I can remember. I'm still just a little unsure of myself. It's probably for the best. I mean, there are some really terrible tattoos that I could have right now if I just jumped at every thought that popped into my head.

Back to the tattoo. A mandala is a circular design that holds some weight in both the Buddhist and Hindu communities. The basic concept is a series of circular patterns that get more and more intricate as you migrate from the center to the outer edges. I've heard some spiritual folk talk of practices where they stare at the mandala during meditation, not unlike staring at a fire to bring about an altered state of consciousness. I don't really use it in that way, but it does look pretty cool. And the mandala is an excellent tool to help me explain how I feel about our next topic.

But first!

Let's put those ten years of Catholic School to the test and see if I can't *learn ya* something.

The history of the Church is pretty damn interesting. It's gone through quite a number of changes over the years, including a couple of schisms that now leave us with a whole bunch of different sects of Christianity. The first Great Schism separated what is now The Roman Catholic Church and what is now the Greek Orthodox Church. There were several reasons for the split. Essentially these differences in opinion from the hierarchy of the Church led to each side excommunicating (86in') the other. The Roman Catholic Church chose to keep their clergy celibate and teach the good word in Latin. The Greek Orthodox Church expanded by translating and teaching the word in the native tongues of their new congregations and also allowed their clergy to marry. There are, of course, many more differences than this but let's not get too caught up in the semantics. Suffice to say, an argument occurred over the rules to which we should live our lives, and then a separation was created. Later on, there would be another schism between the Roman Catholic Church and the Church of England. This was essentially a political power structure where King Henry decided that the hierarchy placed himself as King over the Pope. The Pope excommunicated him, so good old Hank made his own Church. As Mel Brooks once said, "It's good to be the King."

So now, in the year of our Lord 2020, we've got Christianity being religions that accept the divinity of Jesus Christ. But within the scope of Christianity, we have Catholics, Baptists, Episcopalians, Lutherans, and I'm sure a couple others. My mom used to work with a Lutheran woman. I honestly don't know too much about Lutherans, but from listening to my mom's experience, it seems that Lutherans don't believe that saints can receive prayers and intercede for us. My mom considered this a big win for the Catholics. Depending on what we want at the given moment, we can switch it up and pray to the saint that suits our needs best. Keeps things interesting.

But suppose that was the only difference between Lutherans and Catholics. If we went back to that exact moment where the dude who created the Lutheran religion disagreed on the power of the saints with the then head of the Catholic Church; we could basically bring all of the Lutherans back into the fold of Catholicism.

And we don't have to stop there. Let's keep going back in time and repair the rift between the Greek Orthodox and the western Church, we could unite even more of the population into one overarching religion. Before you know it, we can solve these little disagreements and all become one people again.

Easier said than done, I know. But we can dream.

My point about these schisms is that they are simply imaginary distinctions that we create between one person and another. There is a separation that makes me a Buddhist, and makes you a Catholic or whatever else. There are separations that make me a person and that tree over there a tree. But the interesting thing is that if you sit long enough, you'll realize that none of these distinctions really exist.

Let's consider a bridge. Let's consider the best bridge in the world. The Verrazano Bridge. In 1964 it opened as the longest suspension bridge in the western hemisphere (suck it Golden Gate.)

It is famously the start of the New York City Marathon, where runners begin their journey crossing from Staten Island into Brooklyn. So it is safe to say that the Verrazano Bridge connects my hometown of Staten Island to Brooklyn. But couldn't you say that the Verrazano Bridge separates Staten Island and Brooklyn too? At one point, you're on Staten Island, then you walk over some imaginary line, and then all of the sudden, you're in Brooklyn. So connection and separation are matters of perspective, rather than fact. So let's suppose you're reading a hardcover copy of this book (I don't know why but I hate kindles. They seem too impartial to me.) The book is so obviously not you. But the hand that is holding the book totally is you, isn't it? Or maybe it's not. Maybe it's 'your hand' in the same way that it's 'your book.' But sooner or later, you can get back to a certain spot that is simply you, right? You could totally disconnect yourself from the thing that is one hundred percent you, and the things that are 100% not you.

Except that you can't.

'When I seek my mind, I cannot find it.'

33

Language is tricky. We refer to our hand as if we own it. During my training at CorePower, I was given feedback that when I cued during the class, I should say things like lift your leg instead of lift the leg. Their thought is that this small change makes the practice more personal. I took this as an opportunity.

Whose leg?

Their leg.

Who's they?

The student.

But the leg isn't the student?

I continued like this for some time, just to be difficult. "Thank You for Smoking" taught us all that if you argue correctly, you can never be wrong.

But I truly don't believe that there is a student who owns the leg because I can't prove the student separate, and no teacher or spiritual being or regular being for that matter has been able to come up with a satisfactory answer for me. From my perspective, the ego or the idea of "self" just seems to be a way of understanding the world around us. It's similar to language. I write the word 'book' here, but the word 'book' is just a symbol, so you understand the idea of a book. It's not, nor will it ever be a book.

Just like you. Just like self.

Self or the ego is an interesting tool we've found to help explain and interact with the world around us, but it's simply an idea. It's not a tangible thing. It's a symbol that we have to maintain in order to keep the game of life or existence going. The problem begins when we take the symbol too literally. Think, I don't know, people who get pissed about somebody kneeling and disrespecting a flag hence disrespecting their country.

It's just a symbol. It's not the real thing. There's an idea that exists in Buddhism known as breaking the Buddha. When you begin your meditation practice, you may have an altar with a serene little Buddha chilling in meditation, but sooner or later, you're supposed to detach from that symbol so as not to devote your life or your practice to a totem. Same thing with the actual practice of meditation or yoga. Especially in yoga.

34

Too often, I see people returning to the mat over and over and over again. Practicing three times a day or more and just absolutely destroying their bodies. The point of yoga isn't to do more yoga. The point of yoga is to take the lessons you learn from the mat and apply them to your everyday life. The same is true of meditation. Nobody really cares if you can sit still underneath a Bodhi tree for 40 days and 40 nights. What I care about is how your meditation practice has allowed you to deal with the trials and tribulations of everyday life. Don't get me wrong, it's important to push yourself in the practice. Whatever the practice might be. And at times, you have to commit and go a little deeper to gain some better understanding. But the opposite is also true in that sometimes you have to step back and out of the practice so that you can see that big picture again.

So let's return to the mandala as an example. When you draw a mandala, you start at the center. And you start with a circle. Plain and simple. Then you add the second row. This can be another circle with just a little bit more of an intricate pattern added to it. Nothing too crazy but a little bit more than just a circle. And then you continue the process. You keep heading outward further and further from the source, but everything is based on that original circle. And now imagine that this mandala is a great continent. A gigantic landmass surrounded by water on all sides. Imagine yourself sitting at the very edge of a cliff overlooking the waves that crash along your shore. You look out into a vast ocean. You look left and right, and maybe you can make out the closest points that jut out into the sea just like your vantage point.

You are as far from the heartland as you can be, and yet you are connected to it. Your perspective is different than any perspective that exists behind you. And you believe that because of the space that you are standing in, you have the best view of the world surrounding you. You believe that the space you occupy is most important.

But.

The space that you occupy is only possible because of the less intricate pattern that preceded you. And the less intricate pattern before that. And the less intricate pattern before that and so on and so forth until you get all the way back to your original circle. Your original outline and empty space. And in reality, your little cliff is just one part of the entire design. It doesn't exist without everything around it. It exists in relation to everything around it.

The best way I've ever heard it described is by Brad Warner. "You are a sensory organ of the universe that is desperately trying to experience itself." Isn't that beautiful? First of all, it takes a lot of pressure off of you as this individual entity that is trying to make their way in a mostly impartial world that may even be actively working against you. Instead, you see your role as part of the whole. You can see the good things that happen to you as something that this universe needs to experience through your organ. You can see the bad things as something the universe has to experience through your organ. You can see anything and everything that happens as the natural progression of the universe and yourself as a certain perspective of those happenings. A thousand eyes all peering back at the center. Taking that 180-degree turn from your clifftop and looking back at the source rather than out into the ether.

In the documentary *180 Degrees South*, the founders of North Face and Patagonia discusses conservationism and suggests that sometimes the best move you can make is a 180 degree turn. So with all the great schisms that have occurred that show us where we are different from one another, with all of the stories we tell ourselves to ensure our own identity amongst the masses of human and animal life on this planet, with all of the separations that we see, maybe we can take a moment to consider how those separations began as connections. Let's not look at what makes a Catholic a Catholic and Lutheran, a Lutheran. Let's not differentiate a Buddhist from a Hindu.

Let's look for those little connections. You believe this? We believe that too! We just call it something different. Half of those distinctions exist in a language that can never tell the whole story. Remember, the Tao that can be spoken is not the eternal Tao.

I first really took notice of this in yoga teacher training. When we went into philosophy, our teacher expanded on a number of different topics and sutras of the yogic faith. And every time he spoke about something, I would revert back to my knowledge of Zen and Buddhism and see the connections. We had the same thought processes—the same values. We just used different stories to get our points across.

And this is why I, for the most part, avoid organized religions. A great deal of them ask you to accept their faith as the one true answer. But really, they are all different endpoints of the same mandala, and if you take a couple steps backward, we start from the same blank circle. That's religions, that's countries, that's politics, hell...that's people, all just parts of the same mandala.

Chapter 5

WHY I PRAY TO ZEUS

I grew up with Disney movies. My first time at Disney World was when I was four. My mom says I was excited, but I was still so little that by the end of the day in that massive park, my feet were just dragging on the floor. And yes, that is a casual parent shaming to anyone putting a kid older than four in a stroller. In my day we walked. And it was uphill both ways!

Unwarranted parenting tips aside, I think that Disney movies were a sweet little reprieve for my parents from the challenges of raising two kids. Put a movie on, and then just let them get lost in a positive cartoon with a good message as you try to get something else knocked off your to-do list. As a kid, I think I had a lot of spectrum-like tendencies. I say 'as a kid' like they've all cleared up now. Anyway, when I watched a movie, I watched that movie. And then I watched it again. And again. And again. Even as I got older and Blockbuster became the thing, I remember getting weekend rentals where we would watch as a family Friday night, and then I would sneak in two to three more sessions over the weekend, just reliving the story and making sure I didn't miss anything. It's why my reference game is tight. It's why I know the dialogue in important scenes. It's why I know all the words to all the songs.

My Disney heroes are not surprising. Mowgli, Aladdin, Tarzan. Fairly predictable for a little dude who couldn't sit still. But one guy that I go back to a lot now when I think about religion is Hercules.

In the Disney cartoon adaptation of the story of Hercules, our hero begins his journey as a demi-god in a world that he is just too powerful (and clumsy) to exist in. He tries his best to help, but his incredible strength leads him to be an outcast and a social pariah. When his parents see how miserable he is, they share with him that he isn't really their offspring and that he was found in the woods with nothing but a medallion.

The medallion had on it the symbol for Zeus. His parents then tell him that if he wants answers, he should pray to the gods.

Have you ever been to Big Sur? It's a section of California not too far south from San Francisco that has to be one of the most beautiful places in the world. I became aware of this stretch of heaven through Jack Kerouac's final, almost deliriously written novel with the same name, in which he tries to spend some time in nature to dry out from his extreme alcohol abuse. Big Sur is a place where the powerful ocean meets majestic cliff sides in a display of water vs. earth that is really beyond description. At the end of his book, Kerouac wrote a poem entitled 'Sounds of the Pacific at Big Sur.' He tries his best to capture what it is that that beautiful blue ocean is saying as she laps her wave upon California's shores.

I visited for the first time way back in February of 2016. It was my first year living in LA, and my sister and a good friend from NYC had come out to visit me. So we grabbed my roommate and drove up the coast to a little cabin at Ripplewood Resort. My sister had just gotten off a cruise ship and was traveling around America, visiting all of her friends who had littered the continent throughout the years. The Kerouac in me boiled with jealousy that when we returned home, she would continue to travel north up into the bay and then east into Utah. We bopped around and saw this and that. We walked through Andrew Molera State Park to the beach to watch some surfers but couldn't help feel a presence in the background.

Behind us, a mountain stretched up into the sky. We all agreed that we would probably get the best view from up there. We didn't go all the way to the top, but it was still a pretty steep climb, especially for my sister trying to keep up in her 5' 4" body with three men over 6 feet tall. Jokes were made, and Lord of the Rings references dropped. "We dwarves are natural sprinters! Very dangerous over short distances," I could hear her calling from behind me. It was windy when we stopped. Like really windy. The sea level spot at PCH where we had started our climb felt sunny and warm but now the wind whipped around us so that we could barely hear each other speak. We pulled jackets and layers from our packs to keep warm as we sat and rested from the climb. It felt important.

The next time I went was Christmas of that same year. I drove up with my girlfriend of the time. We would actually end our relationship right when we got back after the holiday. She struggled with anxiety and had difficulty getting ready for the trip. I was probably more excited about the drive-up along PCH than I was about staying in the cabin. So when our departure time got delayed, and we wound up driving through the pitch black of Central California rather than the scenic overlooks I had yearned for, and we never really came back from the disagreement. We stomached each other for the trip, but you could tell something was off, and again while we explored all of the regular attractions of Big Sur, we were not blown away. We were even slightly annoyed by the flocks of tourists that pulled their cars over to the right side of the road, stepped out for a few pictures, and then went along their merry way. It seemed….. cheap. So we took her pup and hiked our way into the back edges of Limekiln Park where we wouldn't see another soul for all of Christmas day.

My most recent trip there was for the Big Sur Marathon of 2018. Now, I'm no runner. I mean, I run, but certainly not those distances. I had just helped navigate so many people through their training programs for marathons that I felt like I better do one, lest I be a hypocrite. For the Big Sur Marathon, they completely close off the 26.2 miles of PCH. I believe they give you 6½ hours to run the race, and if you fall behind that pace, they will take you off the course. They simply can't keep it closed down all day. Unlike other marathons, there are almost no fans on this course. They can't get in or out, so the only people cheering are those who are living along the course or staying at one of the cabins or campsites along Route 1. They also place little musical attractions along the route every 2-3 miles. As you cross Bixby Creek Bridge at the halfway point, there is a classical pianist. When I crossed, he was playing Eye of the Tiger.

I remember all the little things of that race. Andrew Molera State Park in the first5 miles with my unnamed mountain watching from overhead. That waterfall later on in the course that I ran backward for a couple of steps to see. The impossible climb was starting at mile ten leading up to Bixby Creek Bridge, and the views got more and more spectacular the higher we climbed. The waves that crashed during that intense and energy-sapping climb compared to the shallow tide lapping against the sand as I came upon a flatter section towards the end of the course. Everything seems a little more meaningful when your entire lower body hurts, and you feel like you might die if you take another step. Everything means more when you earn it.

Returning to our good buddy Hercules...Now in that day and age, you don't just pray to the gods. You can't drop to your knees right before bed to say a few kind words and ask for this or that blessing. No, back in the day, you had to work for it. Today the Temple of Zeus resides in Olympia, and if the Disney Imagineers for this movie are to be believed, Hercules had to go on quite the little quest to get there. Well, I mean, it only lasted one incredibly inspiring song, but the montage makes me think it probably took a while. After climbing the mountain and battling the elements, Hercules finally arrives at the feet of Zeus and asks for his help in figuring out who and what he is. And wouldn't ya know it, Zeus shows up to answer him.

Wouldn't this make a little more sense than the current and traditional feeling of who or what a god is? A god is defined in most cases as a superhuman being. In other words, they are superior to us, in most depictions, far superior. Some people might look at god or the gods seeing us like ants. A more friendly connection that might make you feel a little better on your insides is the relationship between people and dogs. But even if we take the role of dogs, and Gods take the role of people, isn't it still fairly likely that for the most part, God (or Gods (I'm going to stop doing that now and use the singular)) is indifferent to what we are up to? Or maybe takes a mild amusement in it at best? My roommate's dog spends the day patrolling our house. She runs from the front door to the back gate to the side gates and everywhere in between, barking at any perceived threat to the compound. And for the most part, we yell at her to calm down.

Now knowing the way the world works, isn't it just as likely that a supreme god sitting above us hears most of our prayers or barks with a slight hint of annoyance like we just won't shut up about unnecessary things?

Personally, I think it makes a ton of sense. The idea of God as a supreme, all- powerful, and all-perfect being is a little too simplistic for me. It goes right back to my issues with being told that in heaven, everything would be perfect, and I would want for nothing. My mind just can't seem to compute that.

So let's break this down a little further.

My Catholic knowledge of God has told me that he is everywhere. He is all-seeing and he is all-knowing. And yet, the devil is still able to leave his evil mark upon this world. How does an all-knowing God let him get away with it? The Church would personify God as love incarnate. He is also power incarnate, the alpha and the omega. But there is still this little thorn in his side. I can't recall where I read it, but in some book I thumbed through, a believer of a polytheistic religion told a Christian that if their god did not include the aspects of hate and anger and greed and all those other things that we know for a fact exist, then that god is puny. He cannot be everything that you've made him out to be. The language you're using literally limits who and what he may be.

All perfect is another statement that is tough to prove. I assume that your perfect and my perfect are entirely different. And I love that, by the way. But our perspectives would not allow us to agree entirely on what 'all perfect' really meant. And if he is all perfect to me, but not all perfect to you, then he is by definition not all perfect.

43

He can't be. Perfect doesn't leave room for tiny differences, and all perfect leaves even less room.

But let's instead consider the Gods of Greek Mythology. When you go back and read some of the stories of the Greek Gods and Goddesses, it's more like an episode of MTV's Real World than the traditional western holy dogma. They fought and fucked and fought and fucked. It seems like there was not a time in history where Zeus wasn't forcing himself upon a poor human woman or getting into a beef with his brothers or any of the other gods that he considered lesser than himself. I mean, the amount of rape accusations against Zeus alone is enough to make a Republican think he may have been guilty.

So these Gods were imperfect. Knowing that we as humans cannot even begin to fathom what "perfect" means in real form; this actually begins to seem a little more realistic than the monotheistic version. We would probably have to take out a lot of the swallowing children, morphing into animals, and my personal favorite, birthing Athena from his noggin by splitting his head with an ax, but maybe we split the difference and have a non-shape shifting but imperfect God. It's a bit like the parent of an adolescent, which speaks to the evolution of humans and their thoughts on spirituality. The adolescent knows that they are beneath the parent and not as developed, but they have started to see some of the hypocrisy and the general imperfections that exist in their superior being.

Now we have our imperfect God, Zeus. For the sake of this argument, we've taken away some of his powers but trust that he is much more powerful than a human and that he does indeed know this fact. Zeus is pestered with daily calls and emails from the humans on earth asking for this and that. It's a daily occurrence, and just when he starts to make a dent in the inbox, it fills right up again. And I've accidentally just described a scene from *Bruce Almighty*. Fuck it, we'll keep going. Anyways... chances are, Zeus isn't going to listen to every prayer, much less grant every request. It's just never going to happen because please also remember, this is his job. He's got a ton of other God-like things to do that we need not concern ourselves with because our puny minds could never really understand them. So it's not like he's doing nothing but answering our prayers. Your email might go in the 'to do' box and never see the light of day again.

That's just a fact. There's really nothing to differentiate you from anybody else.

But.

Imagine Zeus keeps his office on top of a very tall mountain in the middle of nowhere. Imagine that in order to get to the mountain, you have to first find out where it actually is, and in order to do that, you have to travel around the known world collecting amulets and puzzle pieces from dreaded monsters and legends. When you've finally figured out the location of his abode, your journey gets even more difficult. You've now got to cross a stormy sea, brave a labyrinth of a ravine and then climb to the tallest peak during the middle of an ice storm conjured up by Saruman himself! Okay, I snuck a Lord of the Rings reference in there; sue me.

You've completed the trials. You've done all the deeds. And now you stand before God himself, Mighty Zeus. He probably hasn't seen an actual person here in eons, yet here you stand.

Do you think he'd be a little more interested in what you had to say? In what your prayer might be?

I do.

An old proverb says, 'hunger is the best sauce.' It's true! You've got to earn these things. I guarantee that you'll appreciate the view you get after climbing a mountain much more than the one where you pulled your car to the side of the road.

So while Big Sur is beautiful, it's not the place that I go to pray. It's not the place that I go to talk to God. That place is a bit more sacred for me, and it always takes some doing to get there. The spirit makes me earn my revelations.

If you head east out of LA on the ten, you're bound to sit in traffic for a while, but once you pass that edge of the urban sprawl, you'll probably be moving at a decent clip. You'll pass through wind farms as you get to Morongo Casino and Palm Springs. To the right of you, the San Jacinto Mountain looms overhead. To the left, and up ahead, you can just barely make out one of the outlook attractions at Joshua Tree. Stay east on the 10 and you'll pass tiny little towns that seem to spring up out of nowhere. Quartzsite, Blythe. Weird earthy names for weird earthy towns. The Arizona-California border has a little stopping point where they could check you if they wanted to, but they don't, and then you pass over a mostly calm and shallow Colorado River, in stark contrast from the same body of water that I've seen further east on this journey.

A bit more driving east on the 10 through land that is desolate and dying, and you'll eventually get to the turnoff for the 60. Then it'll spin you into a loop that kicks a bit north before adding a small east curve, and now you're on a single lane highway with nothing to look at but the horizon ahead. Whenever I get here, I always think I'm closer than I really am. It's the only real turn in the whole journey, so I use it as a marker, but in reality, I've still got over an hour to go through train tracks and RV parks. There's also a tiny little church in Hope, Arizona that is frighteningly eerie at night with a single lamp post lit. Just as you pass it you must reach the town's end because a clean white sign informs you that you are "Leaving Hope." When you're driving alone in the middle of the night, and you see that, you might get a little chill going up the spine.

Keep on that 60, and you'll get to a town called Wickenburg. A little cattle town whose main draw is a rodeo that happens once a year. I wouldn't even know this town existed if not for some family that moved out there some years ago. They've got a nice sprawl of land and a big ranch-style house on a street with no neighbors. From the very edge of the backyard and a window in the laundry room, you can see a solitary peak that looms behind the horse rancher farm a couple miles behind their house. That's where I'm heading today.

So I pass by their house and give a slight wave from the highway. They don't see, but energetically, I still think it's important. I make a right at the Safeway and head up a little road with a high school on one side and a trailer park on the other. I wonder how they have enough kids to fill that school. I keep going on down the road over cattle stops and other ranch-type things that I don't understand, passing beat-up trailers in the desert that makes me assume Walter White is back in action. And then I pull my car into a little spot that I reluctantly call a parking lot and trailhead. Nothing more than some circular dirt and a little sign warning you about mudslides and rattlesnakes.

I can see Vulture Mine Peak in the distance. The rest of the way is on foot. So I strap up my Camelbak and lace up my shoes. The first step is down a sandy hill and then a mile or so walking through a wash that gives with every step. Imagine a beach that you've got to walk for miles. Not the most fun part of the journey, but there are big saguaro cacti (cactuses and cacti are both correct depending on if you go with the Greek or the Latin but since we went Greek in this chapter, let's stick with cacti!) There are also these weird-looking fuzzy cacti called teddy bear cacti that have needles that jump off and latch onto you if you get too close. Dogs beware.

I don't see any rattlesnakes, never actually have in all the time that I've spent in Arizona and California, but you'll see some lizards scurrying away from you and maybe even a roadrunner. My aunt sees javelinas (little pigs) all the time, but I'm still yet to see my first. No coyotes this time of day, but you can hear their occasional laugh if you're out there close enough to sunset. Keeping to the wash, it takes a bit, but sooner or later, the sand will end at a gate that keeps the ATVs out. There's a sign-in book that I sign every time I go. Today I just drop my initials, nothing more.

Almost immediately after stepping through the gate, you're on solid ground, but that ground starts to tilt quickly towards the sky. You make a hard right going up the side of the mountain but soon realize that you'll be switch backing all the way up to the saddle. The incline is fairly steep, but if you're in good shape you can attack it. If not, just take it slow and you'll get where you're going. There's really no rush, and no one out here but you. It's quiet. Insanely quiet.

A rest here and there, but nothing too substantial. I really just stop to remember the rocks that I've meditated on before and believe me, there are a lot of them. I've done this hike with the most important people in my life. Truly. My sister and my aunt and my uncle joined me once, with my uncle battling through a recently repaired rotator cuff the whole way up. I've done it with a girlfriend who I loved dearly. We've since fallen out, and I wouldn't say we are on good terms, but I wish her well. When we hiked this together, we were young, madly in love, and in true belief that a relationship spanning New York to Arizona could last. I distinctly remember looking into her eyes at the saddle and thinking she was the one. But such is life. Right before I left Arizona to move to California, as the last act, I hiked the mountain with my two best friends. Rob from Staten Island and Connor from Boston. Those two had gotten me through my youth, and that first year of adulthood, we partied our way through Arizona trying to figure out what we would be like as adults. I remember that hike being particularly sad for me because I knew that the three of us would never be living together in the same capacity ever again. I'd like to get my mom and dad on that mountain one day. I think that would complete the circle.

It takes a bit, but when you finally reach the saddle, two peaks extend upwards in opposite directions. I've explored the right side to no avail. But to the left, there's something you might call a trail, where white spray paint leads the way up a route where you scramble over some unstable rocks.

This is some hands and feet crawling. Not particularly dangerous as you don't hang over the side, but not exactly safe either. Connor didn't make it to the top of this because he stayed with his dog. My girlfriend never made it because she was afraid of heights. I never expected my uncle to make it up with his shoulder, but sure enough, as my sister and aunt and I were sitting on the peak admiring the view, that stubborn old bastard pulled himself up over the side. That guy might bellyache through every hike I take him on, but I don't believe that there is a thing he can't do if he wants to.

But today I'm by myself. It's just me. So I pull myself up to the plateau and take a moment to admire the view. I can just make out my car in the makeshift parking lot, and I try to trace the route I took through the wash and up the switchbacks. There's one of those little government circles at the peak that gives you an elevation and some state-sanctioned information. It really doesn't mean anything, except for those who want to compare how high they've climbed with someone else. A poor practice from my perspective. There's another book locked away in a steel container to protect it from the weather that I thumb through. And there it is, a weak little note I wrote some years ago thinking I was all deep and knowing.

"For those that would seek the heavens."

Sometimes I'm insufferable to even myself. It is an interesting thought, though. Because I mean, that's why I'm here. That's why I drove over six hours from Los Angeles to bum-fuck Arizona, climbed a mountain that nobody has ever heard of and nobody has any need to. I'm here because I've got to figure some shit out. I've got to talk to someone or something bigger than myself and see if I'm doing the right thing and heading down the right path.

I sit down facing the direction that I assume Los Angeles is in. And I stare far, far, far away and try to see. I mean, really see. My breath gets quiet, and my body gets still. I don't ask anything. This isn't the type of question that words can convey. It takes a while. A long while. Like everything dropping off one by one by one. But I get my answers. I always do.

I thought about writing some of the answers I got here, but I'm reminded of my favorite book of all time, Dharma Bums. Japhy lets out a yodel on a mountain top that Sal says he wishes all their friends back home could hear.

"Those things aren't made to be heard by the people down below."

And I think that that may be an important metaphor for your own spiritual path. It's one of the bigger messages that I'm trying to convey with this book. You can read all the holy dogma and study someone else's experience and wisdom, but ultimately you've also got to find your own. This world is filled with billions of different people with billions of different perspectives, and to classify them as right or wrong are just too simplistic. The question is if it's right for you.

You don't get the answer by simply reading. Just like you won't be struck by the beauty of the world by simply pulling your car over to the side of the road. I mean, you might, but that beauty is short-lived. It's almost cheap. No, I think it's the sweat that makes it count. It's being in the arena, fighting through, and having your own experience that makes the lessons you learn worthwhile. Hell, even my miserable 26.2 miles in Big Sur make that place more meaningful to me. I earned every inch of that road, and the revelations that I had as my knees buckled and back gave out are mine and mine alone. But I know them to be true.

If you can step outside into your everyday life and challenge yourself and what you hold most dear, you'll see what works and what doesn't. I guarantee it. The best part will be that it will work for you. It will be personalized so that while other people may argue against it or poke holes in your revelations, they'll never know exactly what led you to that point. They'll never know the journey that you took. They'll never know what Zeus told you in his mighty halls. They weren't there.

But you were.

And you know.

Chapter 6

GOOD AIN'T BAD, BUT IT AIN'T TRUE

One of the more famous books on Zen in the western canon goes by the title *Zen and the Art of Motorcycle Maintenance*. You've no doubt had it recommended to you by someone if you have ever talked to them about Zen or meditation. I'd hesitate to do the same. The book is honestly phenomenal. When its point hits, it truly hits. But up until that point, the book is a little bit of a sleeping pill with a great deal of time actually dedicated to the art of motorcycle maintenance. Which I can't really act surprised about but also could have probably done without. Or maybe it was the perfect Zen point to make. Because Zen isn't all realizations and epiphanies. It's mostly slogging through an instruction manual of the mundane and regular processes of everyday life. That could certainly be it. And now that I think about it, I actually love it. But still, the book is not what I would call a page-turner.

If you do pick it up, stick it out. I put the book down several times, but it always made its way back into my lap. When the book finally makes its move, it discusses the idea that true and good are not the same thing. It goes on to explore how the scientific method catapulted the human race forward. From that point forward, we were able to test our hypotheses on how things work and develop systems and protocols accordingly. But while it offered so much, it also took away the essence of 'good.' I have always used the metaphor of McDonald's. I assume that Ronald McDonald started out with a fantastic burger. There's no way that company developed into what it is today by just marketing alone. It had to start with, at the very least, a decent product. For the sake of my point, let's grant that the original McDonald's burger may have even been good. As the business started to expand and branch out into more and more locations, the recipe for the burger remained the same. They had a recipe for a good burger, so they kept it. But now with McDonald's owning close to 30 billion dollars' worth of real estate worldwide, it must be said that their burger is not the best burger. And that's because it's no longer being made by someone who cares. It's being made by someone making minimum wage and following a recipe that they have no say in.

The recipe remains the same, but the effort and enthusiasm for the process are lost, creating a burger that is less than what was originally imagined.

Let's explore this idea further.

We're going to work backward here and start with the truth. Truth is defined in many ways, one of which is reality or fact. Buddhism asks us to question our own reality and in doing so, we realize that the six senses can deceive us at every turn. We recognize that sight, hearing, smell, touch, taste, and mind or thinking all serve to tell us about our surroundings but can be easily deceived. For instance, I can see a silver Ford Prius driving towards me on a corner. I know that my friend Erica drives a silver Ford Prius, so I create the reality that Erica is driving towards me, only to see the car speed past me with someone unrecognizable in the driver's seat. In the moments before I see that it is not Erica in the driver's seat, I have created the reality that it is actually her driving towards me. I may have started to think that she will pull over and pick me up or some such idea of what may or may not happen. But I have committed to the thought in that moment that Erica is driving towards me. It is, in fact, at that moment, my reality. Until it isn't. When I see someone else in the driver's seat as it passes me by, my reality changes, but my past doesn't. In the preceding moments, I still had thought what I had thought and in doing so, created a false reality in my head. I know I was wrong, but I cannot change what I was thinking. So at that moment my reality, my truth, was false. I was deceived by the sense of sight combined with the thinking mind.

We don't need to go over every single sense, but let's look at the mind and thinking as the great deceiver. If I am currently sitting in my room right now, typing this chapter, I may hear the doorbell ring. Given the time of day that it is and what I know about a Tuesday around noon from past experience, I would expect it to be my friend Hannah coming over to work out in the gym. As I walk through the back house, across the porch, through the dining room and living room towards the front door, that is my reality. I am going to the door to let Hannah into the house. And when I open the door and it is a Postmates delivery for one of my roommates, I realize that I have been deceived by my thinking mind.

The reality that I was living on my walk to the front door was not "true" in the sense that what I thought in my mind was not actually happening. And even now that I know who was actually at the door, I cannot go backward and change the reality of my walk to the door for truth. The moment has already passed.

So your truth is, at best, based on things that you know, or things you think you know, whilst an innumerable amount of things that you couldn't possibly know, whether you want to admit it or not, go on around you. Which makes it impossible to come to just one singular truth for the universe. There are far too many different perspectives.

There's an old tale about five blind men coming in contact with an elephant and describing it by what their hands touch. The one touching the trunk compares it to a snake, the one touching the legs compares it to a tree, and so on and so forth so that no man has any real understanding of the elephant. In the case of the elephant, they could walk around touching more parts, gaining more knowledge, and creating a more complete picture of the elephant. But in the case of the world, of the universe, you could walk around your whole life, and you'd never even get a glimpse of the big picture.

That's an important idea to turn over in your head. That the idea of absolute truth is impossible.

Moving backward in our title to the opener of "good ain't bad." Some would contend that this statement has no validity at all. They might be right. Once again, grabbing from the book Dharma Bums, Gary Snyder imparts the Buddhist wisdom that comparisons are odious to our hero Jack Kerouac. There is no good, there is no bad, there is no better, and there is no worse. It's really just you making comparisons to how you thought something 'should' have been. The all-powerful Rick Sanchez of The *Adventures of Rick and Morty* tells his grandson that good and bad are artificial constructs. The human who decides what's good and bad has decided so on through their own sense of morals and values, which have been created by their own life experiences. The ancient story of the three vinegar tasters suggests a Taoist theme stating much of the same. In this tale, Confucius and Siddhartha both taste vinegar and make sour faces because the vinegar has a taste to it that, when alone, is unpleasant.

This directly correlates to the Confucius thought that people are inherently bad and must be controlled and the Buddhist thought that all life is suffering and you must try to escape the cycle. Lao Tzu tastes the vinegar and smiles because the taste is unpleasant. He sees it as vinegar tasting how it is supposed to taste. Being the best possible vinegar it could be. Vinegar is only bad if you expect it to taste like honey. If you expect it to taste like vinegar and it is unpleasant, then wouldn't it be good that it tasted unpleasant?

I've made this point before in talking about cats. People who don't typically like cats have reasoning that sounds like they are comparing the cat to a dog. If you expect a cat to be a dog, it's probably going to be a pretty shitty cat. If you let a cat be a cat and do cat things, then a cat is a pretty good cat. But you have to let it cat. You can't force it to dog. If you test a fish on its ability to climb a tree, then it will spend its whole life thinking it's dumb.

So good ain't bad, but it ain't true either. Both parts of the statement are inherently tied together. Truth cannot exist in anything other than your own particular truth, and even then, you couldn't possibly control for all the variables to be absolutely certain of this truth. In the same manner, good and bad are constructed by the knowledge that has been granted to us. Something we see as good now may turn out to be the start of some pretty bad future events.

The problem, if we choose to view it as one, is perspective.

Everything exists at a specific moment in time. At that specific moment, you are a prisoner to your perspective of the situation. Much like the human batteries in *The Matrix*, you are shackled by chains you cannot feel or see. And I don't believe that the tiny keyhole of your perspective is enough to come to any definitive statement about "truth" for anyone other than yourself.

Some time ago, I went through a particularly bad breakup. Though by my own logic, was it only particularly bad because I had expected it to be good? And what kind of breakup is actually good? Good or bad, my partner and I decided to part ways after being together for about a year. We both had our reasons, and following the end, we both had our stories for how it all played out.

To hear her side of the story from mutual friends can be quite painful. It's difficult to know that someone I cared for a great deal thinks so poorly of me. I don't believe that I am the person that she now thinks of when she hears my name. But I also don't think that I'm right. I just think that I saw it from a different perspective. I want to take a look at what she might think. Some of this is taken from what friends have told me and seen through her various postings about our demise and some is taken from my own mind trying to put myself in her shoes and better understand how I failed her.

About six months into our relationship, we discussed sharing an office space together. She had treated her clients out of a single room space for some time, while I had always traveled directly to my clients' homes. She had more experience in this realm and suggested that we could share a space together to decrease our expenses and improve our businesses. She then did all the research and leg work of looking for a space that suited both of our needs. I agreed that the place would work, and we signed the lease together. We even took a cute little boomerang video in the building's courtyard to celebrate the big move. Not even a month later, I bailed. I cited reasons like my business not being ready for this step, but whatever the reason being, I pulled my name off the lease, and she was left paying double the rent than she had originally intended.

With this new level of expense added, she was going to have some difficulty balancing out her own rent. We decided together to look for an apartment we could share. We found one very quickly and were about to sign the lease when I got cold feet and thought we should wait. Without the support of her partner in either her office space or her living space, both of which had been offered by me, she would struggle. A bit of panic set in, and we had a major blow-up of a fight. The next day I came to her apologizing and agreed to sign the lease to help support her in any way that I could like a good partner would.

No more than three months of living together, I ended the relationship over a yoga class that I was offered and wanted to accept that was the same night and time as our connection and date night. I chose work over her, once again leaving her stranded.

I had the landlord of our apartment sign over the lease to her name and left her now responsible for over three times the rent than she had anticipated paying for the year when we moved in together. And I cut off all communication.

Is it really any wonder that this woman thinks so poorly of me? I don't blame her. That was the most difficult section of this book to write thus far, and it's because I can't say that any of it is a lie. But much like the difference between a rebel and a revolutionary, it depends on who is doing the telling. So for a change in perspective, let me speak from my own mind.

From the time that we started dating, we had discussed working together. Our specialties were different, but similar enough so that we could treat the same clientele. I had always imagined that one day we would evolve into one of those powerful business couples that are joined in everything. When the time came to discuss office spaces, I was very worried. My business had gotten by in its fledgling stage by keeping my expenses as low as humanly possible. But I was still doing quite well, and I knew that this could help her out on her end. So I agreed and was excited to share a space together. Very quickly, we ran into some issues on how we would go about doing that. I had envisioned utilizing the office two days a week while giving her the other three and allowing our businesses to grow separately for the time being until we were on a more level playing field to try any type of merger. This didn't sit well, and I found that we were far from a mutual agreement. She told me that if I didn't want to work together, then I should pull out of the lease. So I did, explaining why I was doing it and that I would do what I could to support her in other ways. This was very hard for her to accept, but she did, and we moved forward.

Without the support in the office space financially, she would need help somewhere. Living space seemed like the next step, so we started looking together. I thought this would take some time, but we found a place that met our needs in less than a week, and she was ready to sign. I was hesitant, but I remember eating burritos at our favorite Mexican spot, and I asked her if she really wanted to live with me. Immediately she answered of course, and her confidence and the way she smiled assured me that this was the right move. I said yes, but the night she showed up at my place with the paperwork, we were no more than twenty-four hours removed from another fight.

I said I wasn't sure that we were ready for this, being that we were on such rocky ground to begin with, and that's when the blow-up started. This was me again agreeing and then backing out like I always did, and now it was beginning to hurt more than ever. She stormed out of my room, and the next day, when I went to see her, I assumed we were done. But when she cried and told me how hurt she had been, all I wanted to do was make it better. At that moment, I would have done anything she asked. And so I signed the paperwork.

During the next three months of living together, we were always a bit on edge. We would fight about what time to get up in the morning. We'd be annoyed by each other's movements in our tiny little studio apartment. We had screaming arguments in the car. I went and saw a therapist to try to clear up what I was doing wrong and how this could all be better. We had teary-eyed conversations about what each of us needed three nights in a row with nothing being resolved or decided. And when I was offered a primetime class that I believed would lead to more clients in my business, I wanted to accept. I had accepted much more financial responsibility in the relationship at this point and I felt like I needed to take this opportunity. But she wouldn't hear of it. It was her or the class. I would've never chosen this class over, her but it seemed like a metaphor for everything else that was going on around us. So I moved out. I offered to let her stay if she wanted but that she would have to take up the lease. I couldn't afford to pay hers and mine, wherever I landed. Once that was legally taken care of, I cut ties. It was too painful to speak to someone that I had loved so much and had now lost.

There is, of course, a lot more to that story on either side. To hear the rest of my side, you'll have to find me in a dark bar on a tall stool and buy my next round. But here we have the exact same chain of events being viewed from opposite sides of the tug-o-war. Something that really helped me in coming to terms with the ending of this partnership was actually sitting in her shoes and realizing that she was right. And that still didn't mean that I was wrong! The problem is that we create the story of "what really happened" in our own head, and share it with the people closest to us.

They offer empathy and sympathy for what we are going through and further support our side as fact when they've never even seen the other. Again pulling from their conversation in 180 Degrees South, the founders of both Patagonia and The North Face reflect that you should caution each action you take with the thought that you could be one hundred percent wrong. And if that were the case, which action would do the least harm.

And even that is impossible to really determine! For the sake of that documentary, these two men were looking at conservation initiatives that would save wild areas in South America. They had the support of locals on the coast of Chile who were losing their livelihood as ranchers while dams for hydropower went up in their area. But that clean energy fuels the Chilean cities. It allows Chile to step forward as a global power. At what cost, and is it worth it? That's for each person to decide.

That's what we're getting at here. In the last chapter, I spoke about how climbing mountains and seeking silence in the wilderness was a way of communing with something greater than myself. That's worked well for me. I would never say that someone who does not have the capabilities to get out into the wilderness and climb to the top of the peak can't have a similar spiritual experience to the one that I had. But they also shouldn't try to. Too often we compare ourselves to those who have come before us or who are supposedly doing 'better' than we are now. Our destinations are as different as our trails. That's perfectly alright with me. Maybe I can learn a thing or two from your journey. Maybe you can learn something from mine.

But that which we consider to be good is a manner of perspective, and it always will be. Go back to *Zen and the Art of Motorcycle Maintenance* and you'll see what happens when you try to objectify and measure the quality of being "good." You'll run yourself into so many circles and loop-de-loops that you'll be lucky to come out this side of sane....

Or maybe it gets better on the other side of sanity.

Maybe those who are 'insane' are actually incredibly free and no longer have to play by those artificial constructs that society has placed around us. If you want to look at it from one way, at least take a moment to consider the other.

Chapter 7

BALANCE, AND WHY IT'S A GOOD THING...

In our last chapter, you got to see me argue with myself and look at the same situation from two very different sides. It's something that I've done my whole life. If we want to get all astrological (of course we do!), you might say that it is the Libra in me. All twelve astrological signs have a symbol associated with them, but only one is an inanimate object. The Libra is represented by *The Scales of Justice*. The incredibly rational air sign that weighs both sides of the argument and passes the unbiased judgment that a sentient being could never hope to command.

The yoga studio has always been a fantastic place for me to challenge my balance, and I mean that in more ways than one. First off, there's the obvious challenge of being in a million different postures that you would never have to do outside of the classroom. From *Warrior One* to *Warrior Two* to *Tree Pose* and *Revolved Half Moon*, I can safely say that the time I spend in those positions outside of actually practicing yoga has got to be less than five percent of my day. If I wind up in a *Revolved Half Moon* on a random Tuesday outside of my practice that probably means that something went terribly wrong. Yet, I still love the balance challenges. The fear, or at least the reality of falling, is so present that these poses force you into a space of concentration in a way that just sitting on your meditation cushion simply cannot accomplish.

More so than crazy inversions and toe balances, though, my initial approach to yoga was a way of providing myself with physical therapy. I put in six years to get my Doctorate and had this abundance of knowledge of the human body and how it worked, but I was really just spreading that knowledge to others for their own recovery. Because of the work being physically intensive for me, I found that my body would wax and wane between feeling healthy and just absolutely strung out from being on my feet all day. I was too tired to work out at the end of a ten-hour shift, and I felt like my body was heading in the wrong direction.

Enter Yoga.

Upon moving to Los Angeles, I found that a great deal of my patients would reference their yoga practice as something that didn't feel right with the current state of their injury. The hip would hurt in crescent lunge, the knee would ache in chair pose, and the shoulder would burn during *chaturanga*. I spent time learning these poses from my patients and adjusting them with my PT mind until I felt like it was time to try it out for myself. So, I grabbed my roommate with the promise of girls in yoga pants and dragged him over to the closest Yoga studio Laughing Frog. Looking back, it's interesting that my first ever experience came through the frog, but more on that later. We walked in and purchased their intro package and set up in the back of the room as to not draw too much attention to ourselves. As class started, we couldn't help but laugh at each other and our inability to touch our toes, breathe properly, or even do the most basic postures. But beneath all of our joking around, there was something there. Something that I found to be incredibly useful for myself.

What I found was a practice of self-evaluation. If I wanted to get stronger, I'd lift weights. If I wanted to become more flexible, I'd stretch. I knew all the right ways to improve muscle length and power from my years in school. But yoga was different. It was more like getting into a mindset where you'd be performing a movement or sitting in a posture just to see how it felt. In the early goings, just about everything felt bad. The positions were all weird, the breath was all shallow, and I just struggled not to make a fool of myself in front of the cute yoga teacher. Though the more I returned to the mat, the more I was able to make the connections between my practice and my life. If my knees hurt in chair pose, I had to adjust my squat routine, or I'd be feeling it when I went hiking. A wrist injury I had sustained way back in high school would ache if I performed a lot of manual work and massage in a day. So I added certain movements and activations to my time on the yoga mat to address it. For everything that I wanted to do in my day-to-day life, I could run a sort of test scenario on my mat and predict if it would go well or if I needed more time.

It was also a time where I was alone with my thoughts. Unlike my runs or workouts where I'd keep my phone and music close by; these classes were a practice in giving away the reigns to someone else and just following along.

It was a practice in trust. It was interesting to see how I would feel about that trust too. Sometimes I'd leave a class thinking it was the best one I had ever taken. Other times, I'd leave with the thought that my time had been wasted by a teacher who didn't know what they were doing. But even in the times when I was unsatisfied with the practice, I found that the reasoning could always come back to me. A good class? A bad class? It had so much more to do with how I accepted the teaching than what was actually taught. In other words, there was a certain type of balance to that teacher and student relationship.

One of the more well-known aspects of Buddhism is The Middle Way. I, as a lay person, understand The Middle Way as being relatively self-explanatory. Stay in the middle. Don't lean too far one way or too far the other way. The historical Buddha, Siddhartha discovered this by experiencing both. First, he lived lavishly in a palace where all of his needs were met at once, and yet, he still felt unfulfilled. Then he becomes a self-mortifying aesthetic in the wilderness, robbing his body of sustenance and simple needs. Still, he was not satisfied. Is it better to be a hedonist or a monk? A hedonist will strive for satisfaction in every aspect of life. You want money? Go get it. Sex?

Why not. Wealth, power, fame? You should do whatever is in your means to make these things a reality for you. A monk is just the opposite. Swear off sex to become closer to God. Eat only what is needed to survive and take no more than is necessary. Control your animal-like urges, and you may know peace.

In your mind's eye, consider both of these archetypes. First, think of someone in your life that lives for satisfaction. This is your live-fast, die-young James Dean friend who never met a drug he couldn't take or a bottle he wouldn't drink from. Consider the way that he or she lives his life. And then ask yourself if that person is someone that you consider to be happy. These people can reach incredible highs, but more often than not, those highs are balanced out with a certain type of low. It seems to be a way of life that is utterly unsustainable. The high at the end of the chase being fleeting at best and only leaving them wanting more.

Now take the exact opposite. Take the person that has truly committed to a religion or a set of rules or a way of life, and they now follow these rules to a tee. No booze, no sex, no drugs, no meat, no dairy, no, no, no, no.

Over and over again, this person says no to some of the finer things that life has to offer as a means of building greater self-control. If you've ever dabbled in some of these finer things or vices, if you want to take that perspective, then you know that this person is at least in some way missing out on what life has to offer. You know that they've made a decision that may keep them alive a little longer than you (then again, it may not,) but in the end, you probably don't think that this drastic of a commitment is worth it. You believe that they're missing out on something.

And I'm inclined to agree with you on your evaluation of both people. I mean, hell I just put the words into your metaphorical mouth, so I would hope that I agree with what I assume you to be thinking. Neither of these ways of life are terribly fulfilling, nor are they sustainable. There are certainly times where I've needed to dry out, but there have also been times where I need to let loose and stop taking myself so god damn seriously. Cause I'll tell you something that I don't think a lot of spiritual gurus will tell you. You ain't Jesus Christ. You're not Gandhi. You're not Mohammed, and you're not Siddhartha. If you've made it this far in my book without chucking it across the room, then chances are you're just one of us regular folk.

But that's OK!

That's more than OK. It's incredibly liberating!

And here's why.

Gandhi is a pretty cool dude. He did a lot of things that got him into a lot of history books. And every girl who's ever posted a sunset picture on Instagram can probably pull at least one of his quotes from their bubbly Photoshopped ass. But if everybody started walking that middle way, we wouldn't really need Gandhis. And when people start worrying about themselves instead of everybody else, well I think we've got a better shot at turning some things around. But let's look a little deeper at this middle way.

The Noble Eightfold Path to the Cessation of Suffering consists of eight steps of right living. They are right view, right resolve, right speech, right conduct, right livelihood, right effort, right mindfulness, and right meditation. Seems easy enough. I mean, if you can figure out what's right and what's wrong. But that's the kicker, isn't it?

Right and wrong are arbitrary. If your family is starving, it is the right action to steal a loaf of bread. Aladdin taught me that much. But if you're the law looking over that marketplace, I'm thinking that theft falls somewhere outside the realm of what you would consider the right action. Now I don't really think that we have to get down into the nitty-gritty of each part of the eightfold path. There are much more devout and faithful Buddhists than I who could give you a crash course on the subject and would most likely scoff at my rather basic understanding. And that's okay, because remember, I'm not really a Buddhist. But more on that later.

Even so, I think that the overarching theme of these eight aspects is important. Because you get this solid opportunity to look at eight different aspects of life and decide for yourself if you're doing it right. It's purposefully vague. Because Aladdin could now say that he did, in fact, live up to the tenant of right livelihood. And who could blame him? He's feeding the little kids in the streets. That's doing what needs to be done. Not only that but the paths of right living are separated into aspects that are a little easier to follow. You may be practicing Right Livelihood, but are you practicing Right Speech? How about Right Effort? Right Meditation is important because it will lead you to take a look at yourself and ask if you truly believe you are doing what is right. And when you ask that question, you might want to look at the dharma wheel, which traditionally may have eight spokes to represent the eightfold path. When one spoke is too short or too long, the wheel doesn't spin so smoothly. But this is all easily restored if you take the time to question how the wheel is spinning. To know balance is to know asymmetry. How could you line everything up if you never knew they were out of whack in the first place?

So the cycle continues. You behave a certain way, and then you take a look in the mirror. You see where you are strong, and you see where you are lacking. You can break this down in terms of chakras. You can break this down in terms of the Noble Eightfold Path. You can break this down however you want to. But you see strengths. You see weaknesses. You make adjustments to the way you live your life in order to better balance yourself out. You look at yourself in the mirror again, and the cycle continues.

This is where a lot of people get hung up on terms like Buddhism and meditation, and enlightenment. From my experience, the practice is what is important, not the result.

This is not exclusive to the three terms above, as it applies to yoga, working out, being healthy, and a host of other things. I've never been a huge Blake Griffin fan (formerly of the LA Clippers basketball team), but a while back, he had a commercial for who knows what that stuck with me. In the commercial, he is seen training for the upcoming basketball season. The audio has him relaying the message that a coach once told him, that you have to fall in love with the process of becoming great. I often reference this in my yoga classes. So many yogis want to be able to do a handstand or a split or some type of weird posture that will look really cool when photographed on a beach. I don't blame them because I'd love that too. But what you have to find is a certain joy in the struggle of getting to that handstand. Can you enjoy the process of getting on your mat every morning and training your wrist to support you at the base? Your shoulders opening to create a better alignment? Your core training to brace you? Because that's where the magic is. It's not about being able to do a handstand. It's about becoming the person who can do a handstand.

This carries over into meditation as well, if in a more subtle way. There isn't going to be one day where you're sitting on your cushion, and all of the sudden, you realize it all and understand everything. Well, actually, that really might happen. In fact, it probably will, but it's best to kind of ignore it when it does. The reason being that you can't stay there anymore than you can stay high on acid or booze or whatever your drug of choice may be. You have to come back down. So meditation becomes this tightrope walk of sitting with yourself in moments of fantastic enlightenment and the corresponding moments of unimaginable pain. But whichever end of that spectrum you find yourself on at any given time, you know that you won't stay there. You know that balancing is not about pushing as hard as you can one way or the other. It's all about tiny little adjustments to the system to keep you upright. Push too far one way, and you'll overcorrect. So you're really just learning how to subtly adjust as you go.

There is no plateau of enlightenment. It is always a constant struggle to find balance. But there is enough in just the struggle to fill a man's heart. That comes from The Myth of Sisyphus. You may remember that he was cursed to roll a ball up a hill for all of eternity only to have the ball roll back down so that he had to start up again. There is no achievement and there is no goal.

There is only the struggle. But if you can imagine him as happy, well then you've got a good understanding of life in my opinion. So live and breathe balance. Don't go too far one way. And don't go too far the other. You'll be happier for the experience...

Or maybe you won't.

Chapter 8

...SOMETIMES

Wasn't that last chapter fun? A nice little journey down the Middle Path balancing on a unicycle all the while. Welp, in typical Libran fashion, I can't let any of us get comfortable in knowing any one specific truth. So let's now take a moment to explore why balance is a bitch and how it can paralyze you to the point where even the simplest decision can leave you looking like a deer in headlights.

One of the more prevalent depictions of your conscious mind is the angel and the devil on your shoulder. On the right side, a little you in a robe with a harp shows up and tells you how you should do the right thing. On the left side, a little you with red horns and a pitchfork trying to lead you down the path of sin and debauchery. Unfortunately, in most cases, these two tiny versions of you do not dress for work. There are decisions to be made, but right and wrong are really matters of perspective more than anything. It's not the Lord of the Rings simplicity of man vs. orc, but it's more the chaos of Game of Thrones with good-hearted people fighting for the bad guy's side and terrible deviants allied with your favorite house. This is real life. It's difficult. Remember Kronk from *The Emperor's New Groove?* Most of the time, I feel like him. Utterly confused by the two competing paths that I might follow. The deeper they go into their case, the more unsure I get about which route to take. The right side feels right, but damn if the left doesn't make some good points. The problem with balance is that once you are balanced, you try to stay still. Because leaning in one direction will take you away from the other. But life is not still. Life is ever changing. So how do we stay balanced in movement?

For one, we can try to avoid movement. This is a kind of interesting Buddhist-like thought, in my opinion. Buddhism seems to be a little more of a philosophy than a religion to me. It doesn't seem to be so concerned with dogma so much as it is concerned with ways of approaching and living life. One aspect of Buddhism that always appealed to me was the dialect in which it is taught. Rather than being told what is true and what is not, most Buddhist dharma talks or even sermons that I've listened to or read begin with a question. The question may come from someone in the audience, or it may be proposed by whoever is leading the discussion.

Once the question is stated, the discussion doesn't so much focus on giving an answer as much as it disproves the answers that come to mind. I think this is a fantastic way of arriving at Truth. Keep clearing and clearing and clearing. Keep getting rid of things until you can't get rid of anything else. What's left may be considered Truth.

Now we can bring this manner of thinking into everyday life. When someone comes to you with a thought, an idea, a truth, you can question it. You can continue questioning it until they can no longer answer. This will most likely disprove whatever they are saying, or at the very least, cast doubt onto what they are saying. It'll also make you pretty unpopular at parties. For reference, it's this manner of questioning that got Socrates executed. So now, let's imagine someone comes to you with an idea. Let's do this thing. And you're on your little Buddhist middle way path, so you start asking questions. And you keep asking questions. And then you ask some more questions.

And then you start to see that these questions are leading you to a place where you don't really have as much faith in the idea as your friend does. So you don't want to do it. The decision to follow them down this path is not one of balance. It's a decision to go left and forget about going right. That doesn't work for you. So you don't do it.

This keeps happening. You've been a devout Buddhist for some time now. You can't be tricked by the mirage of the world. And if the Buddhas have taught you anything, it's that enlightenment comes from meditation. The best thing that you can be doing is sitting in a quiet peaceful meditation. And maybe you are. But damn. That's not really the way of the world, is it?

That makes you lazy. Unambitious.

A bum, just floating around waiting for things to happen rather than imprinting his or her will onto a universe that they can so obviously participate in.

I'm speaking in hyperbole. I don't sit down on my meditation cushion all day and all night. But I hope you can see what I'm saying here. The devotion to this middle way and balance can make it difficult for you to make changes in your life. The things that you consider 'bad' are not that bad. You learn to live with them and accept them as regular challenges that everyone will have to face at one time or another.

The things that you consider 'good' are fleeting and will come and go and probably aren't worth exerting effort for. The mansion in Malibu and the fast car in the driveway won't bring you happiness if you can't find it here. Happiness can only be found in the present moment.

In fact, the present moment is really the only thing that exists. There is no past. If there was, we could go back to it. We could visit it. But the boy who played soccer for the Our Lady Star of the Sea Lions no longer exists. He is only a thought in my head.

The same can be said of the present. The 42 year old hippie dad who's finally relented to his baldness and allowed a small beer belly to form cannot be visited, contacted, or touched in any tangible way. He is no more real than the dragon that I conjure up in my mind when I consider *Game of Thrones* or *Dragonball Z*. When you understand that or think you understand that, or at least try to understand that, things seem insignificant and unimportant. Then you compare notes and see that the historical Buddha said that all is an illusion, and you start to really question your goals and ambitions. If you ever start to feel like you are balanced in the present moment, you kind of freak out. It's like it's finally here. You've finally got it. All of the boring-ass sitting on a cushion has finally paid off, and you are completely aligned.

So just stay like that. Don't move a muscle.

But that's just grasping at another illusion. Ugh.

The secret to combatting this lies back in The Noble Eightfold Path. Now I don't get too concerned with dogma. I take the parts of it that I like, and I leave out the parts that I don't. I don't believe that I could recite the Ten Commandments from my youth, and I'll admit to looking up the Noble Eightfold Path before writing the last paragraph. Half because I was fact-checking and half because I wasn't really sure that I knew all of them. But the most important eighth to me in combating my balance paralysis is Right Action.

Right Action could be a religion unto itself.

I have an uncle that I hold in fairly high esteem. We don't always agree and I'm sure he's got some thoughts on how I live my life, but I always take his advice into consideration even if I don't follow it in the way that he would like. When I was coming to the edge of adulthood, we were down at the Jersey shore together with the family, and he pulled me aside. We went into the kitchen and started hand washing dishes. Just slowly taking care of the dishes that pile up when a whole Italian family gets together for two full weeks of food. We didn't make all of the mess, but we didn't make none of it either. I know he was trying to make a point to me by us taking the time to do the dishes. He told me that the best way to live your life is to do the right thing. The fact is that there were dishes in the sink. They weren't all ours. But when you see dirty dishes, Right Action would suggest that you clean those dishes. Doing the right thing would suggest the same action. In our language, 'do the right thing' also means get me another beer. But it's always said when someone at the table is getting up. And what's the right thing to do if you are getting up for a moment? Ask anybody if they need anything. You're going anyway. So do the right thing.

And keep doing the right thing. Pulling some more Buddhist quotes out of my ass, "practice kindness. Practice kindness over and over again and your life will be pure joy." I have to admit that I've used that caption for Instagram posts before. Don't I make you want to puke sometimes? But it doesn't make it less true!

The beautiful thing about negating the past and the future is that it makes the choices of the present moment much less murky and convoluted. Let's take a meditation example. A few months back, I was meditating on the beach. Just sitting at the edge of the tide in my lotus posture, eyes open, staring out into the surf. The goal of meditation, if there can be a goal, is enlightenment. Or to make it easier, let's call it spiritual advancement. Moving forward on your spiritual path. A toddler, maybe 3 or 4 years old, walked past me holding his mom's hand. He stared at me for a little bit the way kids of that age will, considering what I may be doing, and then he smiled and started waving to me. So I waved back. Had I been fully committed to the future Kevin, who is all-knowing and enlightened, then the right action would be to ignore him because I am prioritizing my future self. But if there is only the present moment, then future enlightened Kevin doesn't exist and he never will. So, Right Action in this given moment is to wave back at a little kid. The Right Action is to be kind.

Some people, especially people in power, will sacrifice the now for the future. And I get that. I'm responsible for me and me alone. If I had kids, the choices might be a little different. If I was in charge of a large company, the choices might be different. If I were in charge of a city, state, or country, the decisions would be different. But the thought remains that the ends do not justify the means. If everyone simply worried about the means, the ends would work themselves out. I am assured of this.

So I try not to worry about my plan for the future. I try not to worry about the decisions that haven't come up for me yet. I try to make the right decision in every single moment of every single day. Because if I keep making the right decisions, then it only makes sense that I would end up in the right place. Right?

I'm often paralyzed. Five-year plan? I don't have one. Ten-year? You must be kidding. But I can balance myself in the present moment with the right action. I don't really move, but the world moves around me. So even though this precarious balancing act leaves me standing still in the eyes of some others, I still tend to get where I'm going.

Chapter 9

NOT ANOTHER BUDDHIST

This may be a perfect time in our journey for me to bring attention to some things that you have probably already surmised. First off, I struggle greatly with authority. I've developed the practice of warning my teachers beforehand that I don't sit well in the seat of a student. I'll try to argue and go all punk rock, but in the end, if something worthwhile is said or I receive some helpful feedback, I'll bristle at the thought of actually needing someone else's help and then I'll go off on my own to do the work that they suggested. I'm just a bit bitchy like that. Second, I don't really give a shit about religions. Now maybe that's not saying it right. Because one of my biggest fears in writing a book such as this is that it will actually one day get finished, I'll release it and maybe have to give a few talks in bookstores to try to get people to buy the thing. At those little gatherings right there, front and center, will be your all-knowing Buddhist scholar with several notes rather than questions on my misinterpretation of sacred lore. You may laugh, but I've seen it happen!

I was at the Mystic Journey Bookstore on Abbot Kinney Ave. in Venice, California (what a name drop!) to see Brad Warner speak about his most recent book. The crowd itself was pretty calm. Brad seems to attract a reasonable type of Buddhist, and I'll always love him for that. But Mystic Journey brings in some people that don't really have their feet on the floor. He was elaborating on a good question about meditation when a woman strolled into the back and sat down to listen to what was going on. Then after his answer, she raised her hand and asked if he ever meditated. That drew a solid chuckle from the audience who, despite Brad's best efforts to let us know he's just some dude, revere him. She took the laugh in stride and explained that while meditating, you can travel on the astral plane to thousands of lifetimes and universes.

If you know anything about Brad's work, that couldn't be further from what he preaches. He's actually got some pretty good burns for people like that.

Now I bear this woman no ill will (except that deep down I do), but if you're late to a book reading and have no idea what the book is about or what is being discussed, maybe just shut up? Cause if she had a real question for Brad, that would've been fine. But her question was just a foot in the door for her to talk about her own shit. And that's pretty infuriating because I didn't come to this book talk to hear her thoughts that don't concern the book at all. But hey, some people love to have that mic in their hands.

Anyways, I'm fairly scared to do something like that and be challenged by these thoughts that I have. But I'm not scared of being wrong. It's not about right and wrong. I'm not a theologian, and there are plenty of people who have studied these mysteries much deeper than I have. I'm more scared of trying to fake a discussion with someone who is just waiting for their turn to speak. That's called a debate, and if you haven't noticed every four years, it's an absolute farce of grown men and women bickering like they're seven. A discussion is me explaining my perspective so that you may understand and you explaining your perspective so that I may understand. I'm not right. You're not wrong. I'm not the holy one. Hell, I'm not even an expert. And I'll let you in on a little secret. I'm not a Buddhist…well, not really anyways.

When I was in college, I started attending a group-led mindfulness meditation. It lasted about 30 minutes and was held at different times on each weekday in The Sacred Space. The Sacred Space was a spot on the second or third floor of Ell Hall where the religious groups would have their meetings. My first experience there was for an intro to physical therapy class where we all laid down and were led through a full body scan. Oddly enough, that was the last time a class ever made me go there as far as I remember. I don't really even know how I ended up back there again attending these sessions.

I was a little bit lost in my freshman year of school. I was no longer that jock that everybody knew. I was doing terribly in school and smoking entirely too much weed. I napped a lot and did fairly little. It's hard to imagine now, but even the gym didn't appeal to me. It seemed stupid since it wasn't attached to a team workout. I went into a little bit of a dark place, and maybe that's what led me there.

But I honestly don't know. It's not like I remember my first ever class and walked out with a glow and levitating two inches above the floor. It's just something that I did this one time. And then another. And then another. And then it was just my thing.

My favorite meditation leader was this guy named Jason. He had a beard and glasses, your typical intellectual-looking type. He was tall and skinny, and it wouldn't have surprised me if he had never played a sport in his life, not that that really matters it's just how I used to size people up back then. I would later find out that Jason ran marathons. And not only did he run them, but he would also run them with an iPad or something like that and stop every mile to interview people. A stark contrast from me at my first marathon, huffing and puffing and trying to muscle my way to the finish line. This guy just enjoyed the course.

We would all sit in a circle on little cushions, and Jason would breathe us in. He would simply cue the posture a bit and then cue the breath and then fade into silence. Just nothingness, nothing at all, just sitting there. And it seemed like every time I was ready to move or had an itch I wanted to scratch, Jason would chime in with a quick word of wisdom or line from a little book of poetry he kept with him. That was always nice. It would bring me back to the room and the practice. And then nothing. Nothing at all. Just sitting there. Once again, just as I was ready to tap out or had started sorting out my to-do list, he would come back with a line or two.

The one I remember most and use in my own classes sometimes is that of a frog on a lily pad. He sits super still, just gazing out into the reflected pond water. All of a sudden, it starts to rain. The little drops create perfect circles on the clear glass water. Still, the frog does not move. The rain gets harder to the point where the water is no longer still. You cannot make out the singular ripples. The drops are relentless, creating a constant wave pool before the frog's eyes and, still, he does not move. The rain falls on his head, and he does not move. He simply sits and watches the storm unfold in front of him, until the pond becomes still again.

Then after about 30 minutes, we would close out the circle with the sound of 'ohm.' To be honest, I was never a huge fan of 'ommmmming.'

I'm still not sure that I am, though, as you'll soon see, the presence and importance of sound have since become apparent to me. This was my introduction to a practice that they call mindfulness. It worked for me. And it had no connection or attachment to any theology or religion, so I just went with it.

I continued to meditate in the circle throughout college and kept up with my practice as a solo effort when I moved to Arizona after graduation. In fact, one of my first purchases was a wall hanging Buddha at Ross that held a little candle. The remains of the first candle still sit inside the little holder at Buddha's lap. He's the centerpiece of my little altar. Through two states, nine apartments and six years he has been by my side. In Arizona, I'd sit on my little *zafu* cushion on the porch staring out into the desert sky and find myself feeling at ease. No real intention or goal of the practice, just sitting and breathing. But at this time I was doing a little more reading and getting further and further into the ideas of spirituality and beginning my search for some type of religion I could call my own.

My experience with Buddhism up to this point was little to none. The first time that I really got interested in the subject was through

Jack Kerouac's *Dharma Bums*. In his sequel to the historic novel *On the Road*, Kerouac traded the party animal Neal Cassidy for the almost sage-like monk of Gary Snyder. Something that had always interested me about Kerouac's books was his ability to latch onto another character who he held in high esteem, almost idolizing them, and incorporate some of their story into his. Or maybe his into theirs. For *On the Road*, he was the bookish college student when Neal Cassady flew in like a bat out of hell to show him the beauty of fast cars flying across the continent. By *Dharma Bums*, Kerouac had found some Buddhism and gravitated towards the outdoorsy Zen of this mountain man from the Pacific Northwest.

In the book, the two of them climb the Matterhorn of California. Kerouac's brilliant prose connected hiking to life in that sometimes hiking is walking through a beautiful field of flowers and in the next instant it could be trudging through weeds under an unforgiving sun. Such is life. As they neared the top of the mountain and he is too scared to summit, he reflects on how their other hiking companion was sitting quietly in a field somewhere chewing on grass while his vain grasping and ambition led him to where he was clinging to the side of a mountain for dear life.

In typical Kerouac fashion, he travels back to the east coast, and when he gets there he spends a quiet holiday with his family mostly meditating alone in the woods under two pine trees. That hit a chord for me. The peaceful outsider not taking any part in the regular quarrels and up and down nature of an east coast family affair.

The book even has a quick cameo by Alan Watts, though I don't recall the name Kerouac gives him. During their only conversation Watts tells Kerouac that it's all about meeting as many people as possible. That's his Buddhism. In the foreword of the book and countless publications later on you can see that Watts was actually quoted to say that Kerouac had 'Zen flesh but no Zen bones.' Which is a fairly Buddhist thing to say.

So the Kerouac starting line led me to Watts, who we can touch on a bit later, and then some Taoism and some Shamanism and a whole other mess of pagan ideology and just a general path of 'letting the devil in' as the Catholic Church would put it. But still, I didn't feel called to any type of gathering. Any type of church. My knowledge was from an academic standpoint that I was trying out in everyday life, which really is the best way to do it. In the words of Kerouac, "experience is the best teacher, and not from someone else's skewed vantage point."

But there must have been a calling of some sort, because one day I was driving home from work on Pico in Santa Monica and I passed a structure that I passed every day on my commute. For the first time noticed the sign out from. It claimed to be an SGI Buddhist Temple. Underneath the brick was a light up screen that gave times of service and just as I was passing it, it flashed bright red:

INTRO TO BUDDHISM: EVERY FRIDAY NIGHT AT 6

I mean if that's not the calling, what is? I've always had trouble making decisions, but have held true to the thought that if I listen closely enough to the universal flow (a very Taoist thought) that I'll get to exactly where I am supposed to be.

What do you know about SGI Buddhists? Well what do I know about SGI Buddhists? My very surface layer understanding of this particular sect is that the world flows around a vibrational harmony. That vibration is perfected in the chanting of the lotus sutra. The part that I know how to chant, and still do at times goes like this:

Nam Ye Ho Ren Ge Kyo

So you're in a group of anywhere from 5 to 100 people (in my short experience of this religion) and you all begin to chant. And you chant and chant and chant and chant. And let me tell you that if you get enough people in a room chanting this sacred text, something definitely happens. There is a feeling in the air that is difficult to describe. It wouldn't be far off to say that the particles of the air start to vibrate closer together so that you can't see, but you can feel this connection between you, the person next to you, the air, even the bench you are standing in front of. It all kind of just makes sense. I was very down with this part. But alas, this religion had all the same problems that I had experienced in.

Catholicism. Within two visits to the temple, they were ready to sign me up as a regular member and indoctrinate me. If you join, a holy written scripture of the lotus sutra is brought to your house and ceremoniously hung somewhere that you may chant to it on a daily basis. When I started getting cold feet, the very nice man who had been showing me around brought in this woman from Korea to speak to me and tell me how this religion changed her life. She even wrote me a very nice postcard about how she was praying for me every day. I still have it.

I would later go on to read a book called Waking the Buddha that describes the history of SGI Buddhism. It's a fascinating read of how imperialism in Japan and the dropping of the atomic bomb during World War 2 really spurred a movement to create a better world. My problem with the religion is that it seemed reactive. You could trace all of their reasons for doing this or doing that back to something that had happened during those times to one or two of the founders. I didn't want a reactionary religion. I wanted something that was true all the way around no matter where you grew up, what you did for a living and which side of a war you fought on.

I was reminded of my very first time in the temple where I was given a tour, taught how to chant and then sat with the intro to Buddhism discussion group. We went around in a circle where each person got an opportunity to let us know why they were there or what the practice had done for their lives. There was an older man of what I guessed as Japanese descent who I had noticed cleaning up after all the chanting who sat in the circle with us.

He seemed to be either a volunteer or like a deacon or some lay person who helped out. After all of the introductions he asked for the floor and looked directly across the room at me and asked what had brought me to the temple on that evening. I shared a very diluted and shortened version of what I have already shared with you. I said that I grew up with religion, but had lost it and felt like I needed something else. I even shared that I had seen the sign outside and thought that it had to be a sign in more ways than one. He looked across the circle, tilted his head back and slowly nodded.

"Ahhh," he sighed. "So you are truly seeking."

Super Heavy Mr. Miyaji vibes (from *The Karate Kid*). But I dug it. I dug the way he said it and it has stayed with me. I'm not really looking for 'comfortable' or 'happy'. I'm looking for truth. And when you look for truth, you are going to have people along the way that will tell you they've found it. They may have. I don't deny anyone their own personal truth. But so far nobody has been able to put it perfectly for me. Certainly not someone who is backing any religious organization at least.

So I kept looking.

Who I found was Brad Warner. If you've read any of his books, you'll probably notice that I am a bit of a cheap knock off. In a lot of ways that's not intentional. But in a lot of ways it kind of is. He described his practice in such an accessible way for me that I just kind of understood where he was coming from. He wasn't saintly or better than me. He had just done some things that he thought may be of service to some people. People like me. And I'll always appreciate him and his work for that.

Brad belonged to a different sect of Buddhism. I'm not one for sects (though I'd never say that out loud (hope you got that joke!)) but if you're keeping score at home he was a Zen Buddhist of the Soto sect. I'll spare you all the research and testing I had done and give you the cliff notes that this group believed in one thing and one thing only. Meditation.

Now right away that vibed. I had started with meditation. I had none of the frills or dogma of Buddhism. I just had meditation and it had a positive effect on my life.

So if I had been doing well with that but still didn't feel like I needed to add a processional hymn or shit like that but could still use some pointers on how to do what I thought I was doing, this seemed more likely to help than anything else.

I read his books. All of them. Just one after another I devoured the things that he said. He himself had been accused of not being a perfect Buddhist and he owned up to it. He encouraged you to question everything he brought up and try it for yourself. He accepted that his truth might not be your truth and that that would be alright too. This sounded like my kind of Buddhism. I followed him on a retreat to the Mount Baldy Zen Center where he was leading a three day silent retreat with his sangha, or community. It seemed like a lot of people there knew each other but I was on my own. Nothing but a few emails exchanged between the dude who ran the day to day workings of the sangha and seemed to be organizing the retreat. I remember as I pulled up and was unloading my car, Brad's car pulled up too. He got out in a black comic book t-shirt with glasses and a bit of a stooped posture. Not in a bad way, just in a way that you would notice too if you spent six years in Physical Therapy school. I had to laugh. This guy must know something because by appearance alone, and believe me when I say where I live in Los Angeles there are a ton of people in his field who get by on appearance alone, you could tell he wasn't trying to be anything. He was just Brad. And that was more than enough for him. If it wasn't enough for you, that was your issue. Not his.

Retreats are interesting. Most yoga retreats seem to be bullshit where middle aged women sip margaritas by the pool between classes and try to cheat on their husbands. Okay so not most, but no joke, one of my favorite teachers ever in LA ran a retreat that I couldn't fit into my schedule. I was so bummed out, but I later found out that one of my friends' moms had gone and that is exactly how she described it. I was so disappointed! And relieved that I didn't go. But quickly Brad described that this retreat wasn't like that. You didn't have to hate it here, but this was also serious business so you were instructed to take it seriously.

But

And this is one of my favorite buts ever. Like J-lo and Shakira at the Super Bowl halftime show level but(t).

But, at this retreat Brad and the other members of the sangha who would be running the show would not dress in any of the classic ceremonial robes. They would describe the ritual of how to eat, how to chant, how to meditate, etc. but everyone could wear what they were wearing. It reminded me of a friend who once told me the true key to figuring out who was worth that spiritual follow in LA was what do they look like when they take off the jewelry. When you can no longer hide behind your turquoise and rose gold and astrological sun and moon, who are you? At this retreat, they stripped away basically everything except the meditation. As someone who is generally gun shy around religion, I couldn't have been happier for this decision.

Meditation, however, can be a real bitch. If you've never sat before you might think of meditation as that serene picture cross legged on a beach. I've taken some of those pictures. And once in a while you do get that level of peace. But if you go to a retreat where you are silent for three days and spend 5-6, 75 minute long sessions, sitting on your ass staring at a wall, well, you're probably going to have more dark than light. At least that is my experience. Sometimes for those long meditation sessions I would sit down and ask myself what is going to occupy your mind now. And that's not the way to do it, but like I said earlier, I'm not really a Buddhist. So I do adjust the practice from time to time.

At the time I was getting over my fairly gnarly breakup. So once or twice I decided I would roll over the whole relationship in my head and see what had happened. Another time or two I tried to react to every thought of her with love. I even added her name to the list of people we would chant and pray for. Pretty Buddhist of me if I do say so myself. At other times I tried to think of where to go from here. I thought this girl was the one. And then she wasn't. So I played with the idea of a few other girls I knew and their possibility of being the one. That ran through some time for sure. But when you sit for 75 minutes, sooner or later the mind will come back around. It will run away from whatever you wanted to think about to the point where you are thinking about something entirely different.

And when you notice that, you notice that you don't really have control over these thoughts. So you stop going in with intentions or thoughts. You just sit on the mat and see what happens. You don't gain anything from the sit, but you sure do lose a lot.

I do want to share with you a little bit about my worst sit of all time.

It was Saturday night of the three day retreat and I had already played with the idea of leaving early. I didn't like it. Shit was coming up and it was honestly just rough. But momma didn't raise no quitter, so I stayed strong. After dinner, we gathered around the Zendo for our evening session. This was number five or six of the day and I was honestly fried. But you stick to the schedule. I walked in, made my way to the same spot I'd sat in all day, made the same bows I'd made all day, sat on the same cushion I'd sat on all day, and stared at the same wall I'd stared at all day.

By this point of the day, my knees were sore from lotus and my back was having trouble finding, or at least maintaining, good alignment. Meditation will teach you that posture is key. How can you be aligned if you're not aligned? (see what I did there?) So it was a bit harder to get into the flow of this session. But for lack of anything else being able to happen, I got there. I have the distinct recollection of thinking about the angel and devil on my shoulders. They weren't showing up and there was no back and forth. There was just the voice in my head. That voice that talks to you throughout the day. The one that tells you that you should punch the dude who stole your parking spot right in the face. But you don't because you don't really need to listen to that voice. It's just a voice. And you just go about your day with music or conversation or whatever else to tune him out. But there was nothing to tune him out. There was just the voice. And it wasn't a kind voice. It was nasty. It went over all of the ways that I had fucked up my relationship. It had a glossary of the times that I had self-sabotaged. It had several sources on why I sucked. It wouldn't stop. It just kept going. I get exhausted even writing about it because it truly was that heavy. The inner strength that we all have, that voice that tells you just five more minutes when you're on the treadmill, well that voice kept getting weaker and weaker and weaker. Like Smeagol slowly giving way to Gollum, no longer trying to convince him that his way of thinking was right, but just pleading for him to go away and for it to all be over. That voice started telling me we were almost done. We had sat forever so the bell signaling the end of the meditation had to be coming. This is a really dumb thing to tell yourself. Much like hallucinogenic drugs, you really have no concept of time when you sit to meditate because time is just that, a concept. But I kept waiting for that bell to ring. That damn bell. I knew the guy who was supposed to ring it and I hated him for every second that he didn't ring it.

My light got weaker and weaker, just a flickering candle amidst the all-encompassing darkness that spiraled all around me. I can feel it now while I type. That voice is still here, inside of me. He's never been as loud as he was that day but he makes his presence known.

That bell finally rang.

I quickly bowed to the practice and the sangha and the... ah, who gives a fuck. I slipped out of the Zendo, not even stopping for my shoes and basically ran out past the woodpile to a place where I could be alone. Once I knew I was far away, I keeled over and lost my dinner on the side of the mountain. I heaved a couple more times to make sure it was all done and wiped the spit and drool away from what I'm sure was a pitiful face. In that moment I looked up and saw the peak of Mount Baldy way overhead, bathed beneath a sea of stars. You don't see stars in Los Angeles. And I didn't really have them much growing up in New York City either. But here they were. For no reason at all.

I thought back to Dharma Bums. Somewhere in the book, Japhy compares the mountain to a Buddha. Unmoved, unshakeable. Just sitting there and gathering all of that knowledge in a deep meditation the likes of which will last several thousand human life times.

And for the first time in the past 75 minutes, I heard silence. That deep and total kind of silence that only comes from a mountain. The silence that is present only when you take everything else away. I sat down in a more reclined pose, nothing that could be construed as meditation, and I stared up at the mountain and I stared up at the stars. I thought to myself, 'this is my Buddhism.'

I don't need rules and I don't need dogma and I don't need lore. Truthfully I don't want them. My religion, my spirituality, is one hundred percent individual to me. I would never try to organize it into a following, or forsake some of my own truths in order to be a part of one. Buddhism has a lot of interesting concepts. It's got a lot of truth to it, for sure. But truth can't be contained. It's ever growing and ever changing. So that's why I can't really be considered a Buddhist. I just don't fit in the container.

Chapter 10

LAZY, GOALLESS BUM

The year is 2020. The month is March. I don't know when you're reading this, butif you're not aware of what is going on in the world at this present moment, then it was either a big crock of shit that we were sold or you haven't been studying your history book.

About two weeks ago, the pandemic COVID-19 came to America. Since its arrival, we've seen life as we know it slip away bit by bit. It started with the cancellation of all sports. Next, we had airline travel suspended from Europe. Then, one by one, stores started to close in LA as the mayor decreed that only essential businesses should be operating at this time. Tons of people have lost their jobs or just simply cannot work.

The latest order has been "safer at home," where we are encouraged to stay in our houses, social distance from people by at least six feet, and wash our hands like our lives depend on it. After a slew of Angelinos with nothing else to do hit the parks this past weekend, the mayor decided to shut down LA parks and recreation.

It's an interesting time.

I haven't really worked much. Right now, I pay my bills as a self-employed physical therapist and a yoga teacher. Studios and gyms closed right away and as thathappened, most of my clients cancelled their appointments. I've wrestled with new ideas that I can use during this time to keep my business afloat, but haven't really committed to one or the other. I've kind of just been hanging out. Well, not just hangingout. But let me tell you about my day.

It's been a couple of days, so at this point I don't set an alarm. I mean why would I? I can sleep when I'm tired and wake up when I am no longer tired. Time doesn't really mean anything at this point for me and neither do days of the week. So I woke upwhen the sun was shining into my bedroom window. At first it hit my eye and I just muffled myself under the pillows to hide, but soon the room started to heat up and it justdidn't seem like it was going to work anymore. So I rolled out of bed and went downstairs. I plugged a bagel into the toaster, brewed myself some tea, and then sat down on the porch to enjoy my breakfast. I scrolled through some apps and messages and saw that a client wanted to come see me for an appointment. I was not sure if this was completely legal at this point, but he's more of a friend than a client, so if he was willing to brave the pandemic, then so was I.

I decided that the best thing to do while I waited for him was to sit and meditate. I usually set alarms for meditation, too. I'll throw my phone on airplane mode and then sit for 20 to 30 minutes undisturbed. That day, I left my notifications on and sat with the intention of just getting up when I was called to do so. And after some time at my altar, I got the call and made my way to the front door.

The appointment went in a fairly regular fashion, though more antiviral precautions were taken and the conversation seemed to center around coronavirus. He left just as my roommate was getting in.

With not much else to do on the schedule, the two of us went for a three-mile run and came back to work out in our makeshift gym. I began the workout, following my planned regimen closely, and as that wrapped up, I began to mix in exercises that I felt like my body needed. There was no real thought involved as to why they would be beneficial, but rather just something to do with my body. These are the best workouts. Where you keep pushing for just a little bit more for no other reason than that you don't have anything to do afterwards. You want to exhaust yourself before shutting everything down for the day.

And that's what I did. Post workout, we sat in the sun of our porch. By this point, our other roommates had joined and we each did what called to us. Blunts were smoked. Beers and tea were drank. We talked about everything from coronavirus to Game of Thrones to the likelihood of the NBA coming back and, if it did, could the Houston Rockets small-ball approach actually be a threat to LeBron and the Lakers? (I'm not sure it will be, but I think they've got a better shot by doing that then what they were doing before)

The day strolled its way into sunset. No one had checked their phone for the time because it really didn't matter. There was nowhere to go and no one to see with the quarantine in full effect, so why bother? And in a way reminiscent of Walden

Pond, the day just...passed.

This habitual nothingness reminded me of a quote that I once posted on Facebook. I'm not sure who said it and I definitely don't know it verbatim, but it discussed how nonsensical the human way of life must seem to other animals.

Humans create work to do and then they complain about having to do the work that they themselves have created. Most animals simply wake up, move around a little bit to find the food that is necessary for survival, and then return to sleep. Those are the necessities and nothing more. They don't create work to do, they just do the work that is necessary.

One of my best friends at the time commented one word on the picture: "LAZY!!!"

He had a point. At the time, this friend and I were living together in college. Often, on his way to play basketball, he would find me in our living room, taking a midday nap on the futon. It sat just beneath a classic Boston bay window and let in the perfect amount of midday sun. He'd ask if I wanted to join and, as I shimmied around to get more comfortable on the mattress, I'd ask him why I'd ever want to leave this spot.

"LAZY!!!" was always his response.

And he was not wrong. On the spectrum of go-getter to bum, I think I trend more towards bum. Four out of five ex-girlfriends surveyed would relay the thought that my lack of drive, direction, and ambition was a problem in our relationship. Typical Western religions like Judaism, Catholicism, and Christianity reward the individual for their drive and perseverance to get things done. But the religions that have called to me do not.

In order to understand this point further, we've got to take a quick look at the man, the myth, the legend: Lao Tzu. And when I introduce him in this style, I really mean it. There's quite a bit of speculation as to whether or not this guy actually existed. Taoism's most sacred book, *The Tao Te Chang*, was supposedly written by Lao Tzu at China's farthest Western outpost, right before he rode off into the sunset to live out the rest of his days in isolation. Later on, when Buddhism came to China under

Bodhidharma, it was suggested that this new religion was a corruption of Taoism that the barbarians of the west could better understand. This guy is absolutely steeped in legend and lore and mysticism and I couldn't appreciate that more.

In college, during some type of event, we played an ice breaker where you were provided with questions to ask the stranger you were paired with. One of the questions was, "What movie character do you identify with or aspire to be?" I had an answer ready to go and I was actually amazed that it didn't get a better reaction, but what can you do? In the early 2000s college comedy *Van Wilder*, Ryan Reynolds plays a super senior who just won't graduate. When the school newspaper tries to get a story with him, they send their sexy reporter played by Tara Reid and the two share a hot chocolate and conversation in the penalty box of the school's hockey rink. When asked about his lifestyle of partying and general avoidance of graduation and the real world, he offers the sage wisdom, "Don't take life too seriously. You'll never get out alive." If you search the quote online, it's attributed to Van Wilder himself. But go back to the scene and he actually attributes this moral compass of his life to a guy he used to party with early in his college career.

And that's the character that I chose for this little icebreaker. The dude never actually appears in the film. I'm not even sure he's given a name, but he's such a major player here. He had enough of an effect on the life of the protagonist that he was interesting enough for an entire movie. Now, I'm not saying that I want or need to inspire people to become the type of person who gets his own movie or newspaper article. But I do hope that the way that I live my life or go about my business can have some type of effect on the way people I come in contact with choose to go about theirs.

That's Lao Tzu to me. Supposedly, it may have been several different people that, for the sake of the religion, were merged into one person. He also definitely could have been a real person, but the dubious accounts of the age he lived to, his story book exit from ancient China, and his possible return as Bodhidharma kind of make you question the validity. The historical Confucius was said to have met him and walked away, saying that Lao Tzu was a dragon and he could never understand him. Pretty high and mythical praise from China's most storied philosopher.

The legendary nature of Lao Tzu doesn't make the teachings of Taoism any less useful. It may even make them more useful. Taoism suggests that we all have a part to play in this universe. If you play your part, you will be content. If you struggle to play a part that is not your own, then you may have a hell of a time in this life. There are two concepts with Taoism that ring true to this certain sense of non-activity in place of ambition. They are *wu ei* and *te*.

First, let's look at *wu wei*. Translations for this term include "inexertion" and "inaction," but my personal favorite is "effortless action." *Wu wei* is best exemplified by the nature of water. It was the legendary Bruce Lee who instructed us, "You must be shapeless. Formless, like water. When you pour water into the cup, it becomes the cup. When you pour water in a bottle, it becomes the bottle. When you pour water in a teapot it becomes the teapot. Water can drip, but it can also crash. Become like water my friend." This advice leans me to the "effortless action" translation rather than the other two. If inaction or inexertion were more correct, then the water would probably stay in its form no matter the container. But, that's not how water works. Water doesn't really have a destination in mind as it flows down the river. It just has a certain direction that it flows. As it comes to a rock, it doesn't try to avoid this obstacle, but instead it adapts its course and bounces off. These silly little obstacles come up along the path of the river and the water just bobs and weaves its way down effortlessly. Though Lao Tzu is careful to tell us in the first lines of his legendary text that, "The Tao that can be told is not the eternal Tao," we often translate it as "the way." A simple name for a simple philosophy. Simply go with the flow and you'll get where you're going.

The other important concept within Taoism for me is *te*. Te is also translated many ways, but my favorite is "inherent character." To look more closely at this term, I want to reference two great pieces of literature by Benjamin Hoff's The Tao of Pooh and The Te of Piglet. In two of the more popular western books on Taoism, Hoff explores the dynamic duo of The Hundred Acre Wood and just why we love them so much.

First, there's Pooh, the loveable simpleton who just goes about his business and in doing so is loved by all. No brains in that head. Just fluff. It allows him to avoid the overthinking nature of someone like Owl or Rabbit and just go with the flow or the Tao. Then there's his little peep of a best friend, Piglet. Piglet isn't big, Piglet isn't smart, Piglet isn't clever, and Piglet isn't athletic. Piglet is just.... Well, Piglet. And that's *te*. In the example from the book, Owl's house blows over and they cannot get out. The crew is saved only because Piglet is small enough to fit through the mailbox and let them out. It's a job that only Piglet could do because he's just so very Piglet. It's like the saying that runs around the world of dating: "There's a lid for every pot." You could be super weird or what the mainstream media would potentially call "abnormal," but there's nothing wrong with that. Your little quirks make you better suited for certain things than others. The edges of your wacky little puzzle piece fit into the great big picture that is the universe.

I like to pair these two terms. When you can get completely comfortable in yourself or your *te*, then it becomes exceedingly simple to enter a state of wu wei and be at one with the Tao. If you try to be something that you are not, then you are constantly pushing upstream against the current. I'm not saying that it won't work for you. There are a ton of examples throughout history of people who changed their stars and through incredible fortitude and perseverance, are able to achieve goals that may not have been in their wheelhouse. But then again, maybe that's their *te*. To push and to fight and to change the world around them. I often think of guys like Julian Edelman in situations like these. The guy is listed at 5'2," and just shy of 200 pounds. Not exactly what you would call the prototypical professional wide receiver. But the dude works and grinds and hustles and made it his point to do what he wanted to do. I have the utmost respect and admiration for that.

But it also ain't me.

Early on in my life, it *kinda* was. I was a star athlete growing up. Maybe star is a stretch, but it's my book so we're going to keep it like that. I was good, though. I wound up playing football, basketball, and baseball for my high school and was voted most athletic by my peers. At times during my high school career, I was named captain of each one of those teams. And let me tell you, I was a little ball of hate. I often look back now and think that I actually hated losing even more than I liked winning. It's been a while, so it's difficult to determine what I'm now constructing out of memory and what really was (See! No real truth.), but I took it all very seriously. I never missed summer workouts, I ran my sprints hard, and I studied my playbook. I was a coach's dream.

And none of it really ever paid off. I had expected all of my hard work to get me a senior season for the history books and maybe even a few opportunities to play at the next level. But I was small for my sports and struggled mightily with injuries. I got moved up to our varsity football squad as a sophomore and was leading our division in touchdown catches before I suffered my first concussion. I would continue to struggle with them for the rest of my playing days, so much so that at halftime of the second game of my senior season, my coach pulled me out at the advice of my best friend. I had called a defense in the huddle that we didn't run and he had seen enough. I'd spend time with neurologists after that, but never made it back onto the field. I missed most of my junior year of basketball from a broken arm, only coming back to play in two playoff games where I did well but hardly enough to gain any attention. In my senior season, we got a new coach and I spent most of my time on the bench. Baseball had never been my sport and I had missed my junior year while still recovering from that broken arm so that by the time I came to the team as a senior, I was just a contributing utility player. I never hated my job as a role player, but I never got that season to be "the guy." And that's what I had been working for. That's why I didn't miss practice or workouts or jog sprints. I was getting ready to lead my team. It just never really panned out.

Like I've said before, your previous experiences guide your current reality and I am no different. Someone who put in all that work and then was rewarded with their success as an athlete may be more inclined to lean towards a reward-based spirituality and religion. They wouldn't be wrong. Their experience has told them that that is how the world works. But my experience showed me that you can't do things just for the reward at the end. You've got to enjoy the process. Maybe it's because I didn't get the reward that I wanted so early on that led me to have a certain distrust for the gold at the end of the rainbow. Something like heaven makes no sense to me because the reward is too good to be true. The human mind would never accept complete perfection. There is nothing at the end of the tunnel that will ever make me happy. No prize will ever keep its shine long enough for me to not grow bored of it. It will always be the *doing* of something rather than the *finishing* of something.

Zen Buddhism specifically leaned me right into that idea. A teacher of mine always points to utopia as being a thing that only exists in your head. And if you can't be happy here, then you won't be happy there. I took that teaching to heart. I took it as an idea and kind of made it a belief, which is sometimes a bad thing to do, but I really didn't do it on purpose! The problem is that when you realize this, there is no ambition or reason for pushing deeper or further than where you are right now. There is only right now. So just get comfortable with right now.

That's where I'm at (no pun intended).

The things that I could be working for, the life that I could be creating, it all seems like a sacrifice of what is going on right now. This quarantine as a whole has shown everyone just how fragile all of their plans and ideas and work really are. They can go away in an instant. And if you've got heavy plans going in one direction, it must be a real shot to the dick when that turn is closed off.

So I don't know. I never claim that this way of life is good for anyone else but me. I know some close friends, really good people, who could not and should not live their lives the way that I do. But it does work for me. And maybe some aspects could work for you. You can give it a shot if you feel called to or, like all of the other ideas that I have chronicled here, you can throw it away if it's not for you.

I'll still be here. Just doing what feels right for my inherent character and trying to get into that flow of the universe. Just a lazy, goalless bum.

Chapter 11

THE MASCULINE, THE FEMININE, AND THE INFINITE SPACE BETWEEN

Two days ago, I painted my nails for the first time. Well, maybe not the first time. I think I may have painted them black for emo day back in high school, but this was certainly the first time that I painted them in a non-ironic way. Truthfully, I had been wanting to paint them for a long time. Machine Gun Kelly had recently come out with a couple of punk rock songs which were quite a stretch from his usual MO in the rap game. He changed his profile picture on Spotify to one with blonde shaggy hair covering part of his face, perhaps a sloppier version of the emo side part from the 00's. His hand grasps his face in what you could identify as a more feminine manner and his nails are painted white. The look is pretty dope. And this is the man whose last two female partners are Megan Fox and Kate Beckinsale. Pretty good track record for somebody leaning a bit into their feminine side.

It's still uncomfortable, though. It took me a couple of days to actually get myself over to Target to get some white nail polish. And while I was there, I made sure to purchase a few other things so that it wasn't a trip just to get nail polish, even though it really was. I was even using the self-checkout, but discomfort is discomfort and we all deal with it in different ways. I got home and hastily went to work painting my nails. I literally did just that. Slapped on some polish and thought......... that can't be right. Luckily, my roommate's girlfriend was home. She removed it and showed me the proper way to apply it. It wound up looking pretty good. I got some compliments throughout the week but for the most part, nobody even mentioned it. It was something that I just kind of did for me and honestly, that's who it affected the most. From patients I saw to random passersby, it didn't seem to register on most people's radar. And if it did, they didn't mention anything. It was really all just my stuff that kept me from trying something that I might like.

From the time that we are born, societal norms of what it means to be male or female are forced upon us. The point here is not that there are no differences between the sexes. There are. There are many differences between the sexes. And if we look at the sexes anatomically, it's rather easy to distinguish one from the other. What I'd like to discuss in this chapter, however, is not anatomical genders but feminine and masculine energies. Because they have nothing to do with what is or isn't between your legs. And acceptance of that fact could potentially make a lot of lives a whole lot easier.

Let's first look at the feminine (as the feminists rejoice to be first!). I find it interesting that we don't have more examples of the matriarchal goddess when we look back into history, but I also credit that Roman Catholic Church for effectively demonizing the divine feminine as witches rather than deities commanding respect. But working off of what I know, my two favorite examples of the divine feminine are Gaia and the Madonna. The links between these two ideas are numerous, with the most evident being the creation of life out of nothing. Four and a half billion years ago, life sprung forth on this planet. Out of nothing. There was just this ball of dirt floating around in the universe and then for no reason whatsoever something spectacular happened. The building blocks of what we know as life on this planet began to form, setting forth a series of events that would one day lead to me sitting in my apartment typing away at a book that you would one day pick up and read. There was no father figure. There was only the mother earth. There was only the void. And from her loins sprouted forth everything that we see today.

It's not so different from the blessed mother. When I was a child, I went to Our Lady Star of the Sea Grammar School. That was the title that we had given Mother Mary for our school. Kind of like if Daenerys Targaryen had kept rule over the Seven Kingdoms and a school had been named "The Mother of Dragons" out in Vaes Dothrak because that's the part of her they most identified with. Around Staten Island, there were several other schools and churches dedicated to the mother of Jesus Christ including Our Lady Queen of Peace, Our Lady of Good Counsel, and Our Lady of Pity, to name a few. According to Catholic Dogma, Mary was first conceived without sin.

This is a pretty big deal because ever since Adam and Eve, we've all been born with original sin as payment for their deception in the Garden of Eden. Mary was born without original sin so that she could serve as the vessel that would bring forth the son of God. She did this also without having known a man. The angel Gabriel came to her to tell her that she would have a child without knowing a man's touch and that this child would go onto be the savior that we were promised. So once again, the divine feminine is going to bring forth eternal life, without the help of the masculine. Score another for the matriarch movement!

Now let's look at the numerous versions of the heavenly father. We've got the Christian God the Father, Zeus from Greek mythology, Odin from the Norse legends, Allah in the Islamic faith, and the list goes on. Excluding Hindu polytheistic beliefs and Buddhist non-belief in deities, it seems like most other religions will exemplify the father head as both the creator and ultimate judge of all things. It's not difficult to see why. Religion sprang up originally as a way to explain the unexplainable and, at a time where humans were less evolved, the world was perhaps a bit darker, and your place was more ultimately determined by brute strength, it might make sense that you'd believe the physically stronger sex to be more powerful in the realms of gods. Though, how vain is it really for humans to just assume that the next level up from them in the god realm would be exactly as they were, but just more powerful? "Created in his own image" is always a phrase that's bugged me as the human mind thinking it's more important than it actually is. But maybe that's a topic for another chapter.

So there we have it. The feminine represented as the void and the receiver who, in turn, gives life without consideration of self. The masculine exists as the doer and the judge who is infinitely concerned with ego and the self and moving that self forward by either gaining or maintaining power. It's really no wonder why in this day and age, we are seeing the emergence of a devotion to the divine feminine and a demonization of toxic masculinity.

To be fair, I don't necessarily see this as a bad thing.

The scales have been tipped towards the masculine for quite some time and if you've ever seen scales coming back into balance, there's always a little back and forth before a steady state of even distribution is found.

The problem, in my eyes, is that we have too readily connected the energies and properties of the masculine and the feminine to the male and female sex. Take me, for example. What's wrong with looking nice? What's wrong with seeing a specific look or style on another man, thinking that this man looks particularly good in said style, and then incorporating parts of it into my own brand? It seems like a very valid manner of thinking. In fact, in the sports world, where the masculine energy reigns supreme, we would praise a young boy who studied one of his athletic heroes and copied their moves when they got to compete. Looks are just different. A couple years back, the term "metro-sexual" gained traction as a man who likes to take care of his personal hygiene and create a more pleasant appearance for himself. Males were so terrified of grooming themselves and being labeled feminine that we had to create a new word for what it meant when someone did that to ensure no one thought they were gay or anything less than fully masculine.

You tend to see the other side of the spectrum when young girls hit puberty. As girls develop and physically mature a little sooner than boys, they can lean into their athletic endeavors like soccer, basketball, and softball. The girl who would rather run with the boys and come home with skinned knees than dress up her dolls is labeled a "tomboy." In my youth, I often gravitated towards these types of girls because sports were my most comfortable way of interacting with anyone. A few of these girls, who have remained my friends into adulthood, have shared how difficult it was to balance their athletic prowess while still leaning into a feminine model that they may not have felt as comfortable with. Similar to my terrible romantic interactions in high school, it's difficult to step outside the "masculine athlete" and acknowledge another type of energy to interact with.

These are issues that I struggled with through most of my adolescent life and into my young adulthood. I still struggle with them now. But at this point, I can't help but think that maybe throughout my life I've looked at this the wrong way. Masculine and feminine energies do not, and should not, imply man or woman.

Because to think that male is devoid of feminine energy and female devoid of masculine is simply untrue.

One of my former partners suggested early in our relationship that I read a book titled *The Way of the Superior Man* by David Deida. The book took an in-depth view of how the masculine and feminine energies can interact and balance each other in a way that leaves both sides of the equation providing what they can and receiving what they need. From the very first chapter, the author makes a point in stating that these energies do not refer to the sexual identities that they are most often associated with and that the concepts discussed in the book could relate to heteronormative or homosexual relationships. Furthermore, it stated that even in a heteronormative relationship the partner displaying a more masculine energy did not have to be the man, nor was the feminine energy reserved for the female alone. It could be either or. In most cases, a person does not display one energy alone.

They are often a mix or a blend or somewhere on the spectrum of the two energies.

What is important for a relationship to work is that these spectrums balance each other out. For example, a woman who presents slightly more masculine, let's say a 60/40split, would do best with a partner, be it male or female or anywhere else on the spectrum, who splits 40/60 masculine/feminine. Two partners who identify highly with their masculine energies would most likely clash often in a relationship filled with fire and spice. Two feminine energies would most likely become resentful of each other because their partner would not take the reins quite as often as they would like.

You can see such a dynamic relationship in the typical portrayal of the perfect American family. Let's excuse the fact that this is, of course, outdated for this age and that everyone is capable of breaking through the restraints that we see as gender-conforming roles. But let's also recognize that this is an image that most of us grew up with. We have a husband who is a businessman. He goes to work where he runs his company, is in charge of a slew of employees, and generally is in charge all day long.

After being at work all day and embodying his divine masculine energy, he wants to get home and be taken care of. So when he gets home, his loving wife has created a beautiful meal for him to sit and enjoy, thus taking care of her man.

His phone rings because something has gone wrong at the office the second that he left and she strictly tells him that there is no business at the dinner table. In this moment, in this setting, she has taken the reins in a more masculine way and he shifts into a more feminine role. She makes the rules here because she knows what is best for him. Now some men squirm at the idea of being feminine, but really what's wrong with being taken care of or pampered? I'll sign up for that in a minute. Especially if it's coming from a loving partner.

My point here is that feminine and masculine energies are an ever-evolving dance. They exist as a balance between two people and, as we discussed earlier, balance isn't a state that you reach but an act that you perform. Even when you are unaware of it.

In my own experience, the balance of masculine and feminine energy has not come easy. I often hear the women I teach yoga with discuss taking down the patriarchy and how it has oppressed them for some time. I don't debate that. And I'll never know what it's like to be a woman where history shows that they have been treated as the lesser of the two sexes throughout the ages. But I do like to point out that the patriarchy, as they like to put it, has affected us all. Not just women. Not just minorities. Not just gay men who didn't feel comfortable coming out. Not just non-binary individuals who constantly find themselves balancing their energies in a world that tells them they should choose one. Not just transgender individuals who live a large part of their life knowing that they are not who they appear to be to everyone else around them. But everyone. And there are different layers of being affected. This is not my victim story and this is not meant to be a comparison to anyone else's story. It's just what I experienced. I share it so that it might hit somebody who feels the same.

In the summer of 2018, I attended my first music festival. I had just started dating a lovely woman who was far into that scene, so we decided we would trek up north to the Lightning in a Bottle Festival for five days of music, drugs, and general shenanigans. A side note that is rather funny when I look back on this is that I had known my partner for a fairly long time before we started dating.

And truth be told, I wasn't a fan. I'm rubbed the wrong way by the use of social media in the yoga community, especially by the female instructors pairing half-naked pictures with captions pertaining to the deep spirituality of the practice. But maybe I'm just jealous that my half-naked posts don't get the same amount of likes. I had found her page to be a little self-righteous in writing while clearly utilizing sexuality to attract visitors to the page. And yet, it was actually one of those pictures that drew me in and wound up opening me to the thought that there might be more to this cute Instagram yogi. The picture was of her in a sexy black one-piece in a split at Santa Monica Beach. She had a flirtatious little look out of the corner of her eye, which I would become very familiar with in time. The post, for once, actually paired with the picture. It was all about sexuality. In the post, she spoke about identifying as bisexual.

Now any red-blooded American boy reads that and goes straight to the threesome idea, and I'm not going to lie and say that this did not cross my mind. But there was more. She put it much more succinctly than I can as I paraphrase, but in essence, she said that although she identified as bisexual, she really didn't feel that way. She was just using the language that was available to her. She could be with men, she could be with women, she could be dominant with submissives, or submissive with dominants, and she saw the whole sexual identity spectrum as an ever-evolving entity that resisted our urge as humans to categorize and box into neat and tidy little spaces. She could be anything depending on the situation. And that's what I vibed with. I didn't really know where I was at the moment, but I knew there was more to me than "straight." And this beautiful woman seemed to have some idea of what might be there.

At the festival, I was exceedingly nervous. I had never been to one. I had had some interesting experiences with psychedelics, some of which had gone fantastically well and others absolutely horrific. We'd only been dating about three months and this was the longest amount of time we'd be spending together. And we were doing it as two fairly introverted individuals at a festival of 37,000 people. We were each other's lifelines. I also have a habit of confusing excitement and anxiety.

The physiological properties are very similar. I've heard the only difference is that excitement is thinking about what will go right and anxiety is thinking about what will go wrong. So nerves were high, on my part at least, and I wasn't too sure what to expect.

But all worries were calmed on our first night. Daytime and nighttime at a festival are two different animals. As the sun sets and the countless wooks, hippies, and burners howl from the top of Meditation Mountain, you fade into dusk and find yourself in a nocturnal wonderland of lights and sound. The outfits jump up a notch and heads assume their innermost personalities of wizards and fairies, demons and angels, mermaids and magicians. It's truly a spectacular site to see a bunch of kooky adults playing pretend for the night.

We were no different. I sported baggy black harem pants that swung low beyond my knees and a hood attached to just the arms of a sweater, connected at the middle with a gold chain so that my entire chest and back was bare. I paired this with a multicolored buff headband and strobe headlight that blinks different colors around my chest or forehead depending on where it found itself in the given moment. She donned a black onesie with a full anatomically-correct skeleton on the front and back. Thigh high socks with a femur, fibula, and tibia hugged her lower half. And a top hat sat upon her head, giving the look of a sexy mad hatter out for a night of debauchery. We looked good. At least one person that we spoke to on our rounds that night referred to us as "the hot yoga couple." As a vain and self-interested Libra, I must say that it felt pretty good.

And the evening was pretty perfect. We ran from stage to stage, enjoying the different DJs and getting lost in the art installations scattered throughout the grounds. We spoke with anyone and everyone who dared listen to us and found some quiet time curled up in a hammock together underneath the lights. I really remember the dancing. We were both filled to the brim with social lubricants and, for probably the first time since we had begun our romance, we leaned in all the way and let each other see exactly what was there. We played at the Beacon Stage for hours, admiring other costumes, grooving around the dance floor, and just enjoying each other's energy. We ended the night curled up together in a tent happy as could be.

The next morning we woke up intertwined in that perfect morning embrace that anybody who has loved somebody knows. We cuddled and doted on each other until she asked if she could ask me something. And she prefaced this by saying the question might make me mad. She was already halfway there, so why not ask? She asked if I had ever fantasized about gay sex. And the answer came out of my mouth before I even considered the question.

"No."

It's a time-honored response from the adolescent male. Years of locker room jokes about being a fag prepare you to react to anything that goes against you as an alpha male with the sincerest negation, most likely to be followed up with an insult to the initiator for being one himself. I asked her why she asked and she wouldn't tell me. She probably saw the wounded masculine energy in me and thought best not to poke it with reasons why she had considered me anything but 100% straight.

But then she went to work at the festival's healing tent and I went out to explore. I was alone with my thoughts for half the day while she worked and then the other half while I worked and she rested. Time in solitude allows you to think. It allows you to roll over that initial reaction in your mind over and over again. It allows you to question why you would respond like that so quickly when you knew the answer to be a lot more gray than the black and white answer you gave. Leaving space between an event and my response has been one of the greatest lessons that the universe has taught me through meditation.

The truth is that I had had more than fantasies. At that point, I'd already had experiences. In truth, I had kept them pretty well hidden. The college experimentation phase that women are afforded does not hold up for men. You don't try this or that. If you do this, then you are that. There's not really any room for discussion. Time with another man made you gay. Since I had never thought of myself as gay, and considered some of these urges to be curiosities or passing fancies, I wasn't open about them. I didn't want these thoughts to identify me in the eyes of my peers. So my experimentation was in the dark.

And there was still something about that Instagram post she had made that attracted me to her in the first place. Most boys in my demographic have their first sexual experience with a copy of Sports Illustrated Swimsuit Edition. Impossible beauties staring back at you in barely there bikinis, stirring those early feelings of lust down below. There's a certain worship to it. So I don't find it all that surprising that the thought of submitting to beautiful women in a kink or power-exchange dynamic had also appealed to me. The fantasies that had run through my head as a kid seemed so much more than what early adolescent sexual adventures could live up to. Hours and hours spent pining over a beautiful girl in class and when she was finally in your presence, you jump right to lights off, drunken humping that's over before it started? No, that didn't really do it for me. I wanted to be with that divine feminine. I wanted to serve her. That felt sexy.

And that was in direct contrast to the idea of an alpha male taking what he wanted without regard for those around him. But it's what I wanted. The ability to be in the presence of the divine feminine who was one hundred percent in her Goddess, knowing what she wanted and how to use her servant to get it. It was submissive, but in a way that was specific to her rather than an identification that followed me throughout all of my other endeavors outside of the bedroom.

It puts you into a whole nuanced realm of more terminology that would make your head spin. Am I *demisexual*? Pansexual? Queer? Hetero-flexible? These words started popping up for me quite a lot once I admitted to my partner that I did have occasional interest in men, but none of them really helped. The term that I like more than anything was "open," meaning that I didn't really know what I was. None of the words were working for me, but I'd know what I liked when I saw it. When I felt it. When I was in it. I considered myself open and available to the idea that I was not identifying with "the norm."

At times, I've tried to push it further so that I can discover more about myself, but that has often been met with disaster. The universe tends to unfold as it should, so these days I just tend to leave it be and do things when and if I feel called to do them. I'll forever be grateful to my partner for asking the hard question. She provided a safe haven for me to work through some of my feelings, emotions, and resistances towards sexuality that I had previously avoided. I had never felt comfortable to look into or really consciously explore this energy before I had her as my rock.

But I also think she misunderstood some of what I was going through at the time. Although she never told me what caused her to ask the question, I have a hunch that it was the way that I had behaved out on the dance floor. We had never raved together and for the first time, we were primed with some party favors that let our inhibitions loose and allowed us to hit the floor any way that we wanted to. And dancing is a feminine act. Before you get all up in arms about the incredible strength and athletic prowess of a male dancer, let me tell you that I agree with you. I've treated several dancers and they are some of the greatest athletes I've ever seen. But the movement, the presentation, the pairing with music, all of that sits into a feminine energy. I have no doubt that if placed on a basketball court or football field where the dynamics of the game and power struggle are inherently more masculine, these talented athletes would be able to hold their own. But their sport or performing art is all about presentation. Perhaps my ability to let go and really embrace that feminine energy for the first time opened her eyes to a side of me that she had not seen before. Maybe it was a side that suggested I may want to be held rather than be the one who holds. Maybe I would want to be supported rather than be the support. It's impossible for me to say what she saw or what it made her think, but I think it may have led her to make assumptions about the rest of my life that were untrue and ultimately led us down a dark road that we could not come back from.

Because a man wanting to be held does not make him feminine. It may be a more feminine moment where he feels safe enough to let down his masculine guard, but it does not identify him as a whole. Even recently when Harry Styles donned a ball gown on the cover of *Vogue*, some people jumped to the internet to say how awful this was for a man to be so openly feminine. In response, others ran to their laptops to shout back that there was nothing feminine about this. And I think both sides are wrong. Harry Styles putting on a dress is feminine. Let's not try to say that it's a masculine act. But Harry Style having a feminine moment does not take away his masculinity. If anything it adds to it. Because it wouldn't make sense for him to be on the cover of *Vogue* with dirty jeans and a mud-stained face fresh from a work day. No, it was a magazine about beauty and he leaned into his feminine side and did the most beautiful thing that he could think of.

This doesn't make me think that he can't change a tire, it just makes me think that while wearing that dress, he probably wasn't looking to change one. He had leaned completely into the feminine at that moment, but it's unfair for any of us to take this one instance and make our judgements about who or what he is. That mystery is his to share with whoever he deems worthy of it.

And I think my partner's assumptions of my feminine energy or submissive tendencies went to her head in a way that changed our relationship. The dance of balancing our energies was over as she tried to instill her more dominant or alpha nature through different facets of our life. That's why straight men are afraid of acknowledging their feminine side, as if it were a weakness that others would jump to capitalize on. But this rigid and unmoving masculine ideal is unsustainable at best.

Even in ancient Celtic tribes, it was said that a man must first learn to dance with the wind before he could lead with the sword. Both energies were very necessary for a capable ruler.

Maybe that's the key to all of this. We as humans are constantly trying to categorize and organize a world that repeatedly resists any attempt to do so. We started with straight and gay, and wound up adding a slew of letters to the equation and creating the LGBTQ banner for others to rally around when those two identifications were not enough. But the identifications themselves are no better descriptions for who or what you might be than when the word "book" could describe paperbacks, eBooks, or hardcovers. There's just so much more in all of us waiting to be explored by those we let into our personal worlds.

I've spent time identifying as straight. It evolved to the term bisexual and shifted to heteroflexible as I learned that word existed. Since then, I think I'm closer to queer than anything else available, but the real word that I like is open. In the same way that I'm not Catholic or Buddhist, I refrain from a hard and fast rule pertaining to my sexuality. It leaves more space to explore and simply be. It leaves more space for

Kevin, who avoids labels like the plague.

Chapter 12

THE CONUNDRUM OF THE MALE YOGA TEACHER

When I first began teaching yoga, there was one other male teacher at the studio. At first, I didn't like him. Come to think of it, that happens a lot. Most of that has more to do with my own approach to male companionship and bonding than it ever had to do with him, but you'll see that soon enough. He was about my height with a thick hippie beard and long, dark, Fabio-length hair. It wasn't a hot studio, but still he taught every class with his shirt off. He had a manner of walking in the door, seeing the students sitting in the waiting room preparing for his class, and offering up an emphatic, "Hey, ladies," with a huge smile. I basically thought he was a tool. A complete caricature of everything in the yoga world that I despised as someone trying to play a certain role for the masses.

We'd run into each other here and there, mostly in passing at the studio. Everyone I talked to seemed to have a different opinion of him. One particularly stuck up teacher would say that she cringed every time he entered the room, thinking him the epitome of toxic masculinity. Another student laughed at all of his antics the way an Irish grandmother laughs at her first grandson getting into trouble around town. The term "scamp" comes to mind. But he and I were friendly, if nothing else. There wasn't really much more to say about our interactions.

Now I can't recall how this all came together, but one evening there was going to be a full moon and super clear skies. I had gotten into the practice of somewhat regular sunrise hikes and I thought that on this particular night I could begin even earlier than I typically did, guided by the light of the moon all the way up the trail so that I could see the sunrise in its entirety. Again, I can't really remember how it came to pass that he would be joining me, but the plan was set and he picked me up around 3:00 a.m. in his truck and we made our way to the trailhead.

Hikes are great for getting to know someone. Like, really getting to know them. You'll be on the trail for a while with nothing but conversation. I think this is why I love to hike by myself. The conversations in my head run wild. But when you bring someone else with you onto the trail, you might find quite quickly that this person may not be one of your people. I'll admit that I thought this could be one of those times. I wasn't really sure what to expect, but the moon was out and the trail was quiet, so how bad could it really be?

And it was anything but that.

Over the course of the next few hours and our steady ascent up canyon trails and empty fire roads, we cut it up about everything under the sun. We worked through past relationship troubles with the other listening intently, providing their own insights on the situations presented. We talked about the yoga studio, teachers we liked, and teachers we didn't. We each shared what yoga meant to us and how we approached it as both teachers and students of the ancient art. And we talked about women. Two male yoga teachers in Los Angeles? Yeah, we talked about women quite a bit.

Maybe you've seen the Netflix documentary on Bikram. I couldn't sit through more than fifteen minutes of it bugged me so much. But you no doubt know the story. The footnotes are that this dude who was a yoga champion in India (whatever yoga champion means?) came over to America and made a very lucrative career out of his form of yoga. He created a yoga college and branded his style of yoga into a business model. During his time as a teacher, it would seem that he took several liberties with some of his students unbefitting such a great and powerfully enlightened yogi. The power dynamic he had created was one such that the students in question did not feel that they had the power to deny his advances and were taken advantage of. Since these allegations have come out, Bikram has fled the country and most of the yoga community have rebranded "Bikram yoga" into names like "Hot Power Fusion" at CorePower and "the Hot 27" at Hot 8 Yoga.

Pair this with the "Me Too" movements of recent years and the "down with the patriarchy" viewpoint of some of the more militant feminists, and the role of male yoga teacher becomes one where, let's just say, you tread a little lightly. And let's take a moment to realize that this is for the best.

The pendulum has to swing back into balance. But I think we can also discuss the different perspectives and roles that eventually create such unhealthy relationships.

From the very beginning of the documentary, you can see that Bikram carries himself with some degree of power. There is an approach and language that suggests he knows something that you don't and more than that, he can lead you there. There are several steps taken to ensure that this mysticism or the godliness of him as the all-knowing teacher is maintained. The show actually reveals that in classes where room temperatures raised upwards of 100 degrees, he would sit on his literal throne at the front of the room and cool air would be pumped in through just a couple of hidden vents to keep him cool. This would give him the appearance of thriving in an otherworldly environment where his students were pushed to their limits and sometimes found them.

At one point, footage shows him prompting the class, "You all know the rules.

It's my way…"

They all answer in unison, "Or the highway."

I remember this from football camp as a high school kid. It's a good way to keep kids who don't know any better in line. But it doesn't work for adults. This is how cults are formed. When people or students who are looking for help, wisdom, or deliverance give up their own intuition and choice and take on those of one singular leader... well, things can get pretty messy. You're starting to see my distrust of organized religion, or just organization in general, come out again.

When I was in my yoga teacher training, we dedicated some time to discussing this topic. The power dynamic of teacher to student is one that must be addressed. There are different ways to view this dynamic, as we'll get to, but you must at least give it some real thought. The general thought of the teacher running our training as well as most of the students in the training, was that a relationship forming from this initial teacher-student dynamic was not alright. Interestingly enough, the teacher who ran this class would wind up dating a student and seems to be in a fairly healthy relationship as far as I can tell. Always a little easier to judge the hypothetical situation, I guess.

Back to my friend on the trail. As we walked and we talked, there were a couple of students from our studio who came up. These students happened to be beautiful women. Now, I know who I am. And I've always loved women. The last chapter opened up the idea that I may like more than that as well, but this part I'm sure of. One of the cooler aspects of a yoga studio is that the ratio almost always swings in favor of more women and less men. Anybody who's ever tried to get their buddies into a frat party, bar, or club knows that this ratio does indeed matter. And if you're a woman reading this, just acknowledge that this is a situation where you have the upper hand. It's not a 25% wage gap, but take a win where you can get one.

At this point, I was still a fairly new yoga teacher. I hadn't had the time in the studio that my friend had. I was still a bit awkward and unsure of myself in the front of the class so it's not really like I was attracting all my female students like bees to honey. My friend on the other hand was. He taught two prime-time classes during the week that were filled to capacity, mainly with fit and attractive women. As we walked and talked about this and that, he freely admitted to dates and extracurriculars with his students. It had happened more than once and it would continue to happen, he said with a smile. And he saw nothing wrong with that. And I'd like to take a moment to defend him and his method of thinking.

One of the Buddhist precepts states that you promise not to misuse sexuality. The promise is purposefully vague. It leaves you room to make your own decisions into what is right and what is wrong. And they are your decisions. No one else's. You can't hide behind some archaic dogma to justify or demonize your deeds. My friend told me that he didn't see himself as any type of spiritual guru. He saw himself as a fitness instructor who taught a badass workout class in the form of yoga. Later on when I would take his class, I saw exactly what he meant. He had a positivity about him that made you want to push yourself rather than dread it, but not once did he lean into the role of guru or "holier than thou art." It just wasn't his style. In his mind and in his explanation, he really saw no power dynamic to his class that would put him in the wrong for fraternizing with his students. They were empowered in his class. They felt strong in his class.

They felt sexy in his class. If that led them to express that strength and power in shooting their shot with him after class, he welcomed it.

Now, though I'd defend him to anyone, I don't personally agree with all aspects of this. Teacher-student relationships exist as a power dynamic whether we want to admit it or not. But this isn't about me and my thoughts on those types of relationships. Yet, right now it's about him and his feelings. And this guy was and still is 100% comfortable with the decisions he makes. It's not like the drunk who blames his sexual escapades on the amount of beers he consumed. He's owning what he is doing. Within the realm of misusing sexuality, he isn't. It's not a decision for you or I to make for him. He has to make it for himself and he has. He can sleep easy knowing this.

My feelings on the subject are a bit muddled. As I said above, I do think that there is some small power dynamic in every teacher-student relationship that should not be overlooked. Though when we really consider it, every relationship has some sort of power dynamic to it that can be viewed as either healthy or unhealthy based on a matter of perspective. Because teachers and students are simply roles that we play in a given interaction. I don't think that dynamic has to follow us once we have stepped outside of the designated space where that dynamic was created, and in the case of yoga, the yoga studio. I also don't think that the power of a power dynamic is completely stagnant.

We're going to run completely off track for a moment to make this point. One of the greatest movie trilogies of all time is *Kung Fu Panda.* At the very least, it has to be the best animated *Kung Fu* trilogy with a heavy panda focus. Hands down. *Po*, our lovable panda, is proclaimed the Dragon Warrior by what the stern *Master Shifu* sees as a universal accident. His own teacher, *Master Oogwey*, reminds him that there are no accidents. *Master Shifu* then tries to train this hopeless panda in the ways of Kung Fu. And proceeds to fail miserably. He finds this pupil impossible to train in the ways that he has trained his other students, realizing that he must take a different course of action here. He must treat this pupil as an individual and institute a new protocol of training to bring out the best in him. In the second installment of the trilogy, *Master Shifu* tells *Po*, now an accomplished Kung Fu warrior, that there is always something new to learn, even for a master. In the third installment of the trilogy, *Master Shifu* steps aside to allow *Po* to train the other Kung Fu warriors of the temple, telling him that teaching is the next part of his journey.

In both the instance of *Master Shifu* learning how to teach *Po* in a new way and in Po trying to teach others what he has already learned, you realize that the teacher side of the relationship is learning just as much as the student side. As long as they can drop their ego and get out of their own way. I've come to realize this truth in my teaching as well. Taking steps forward in my path as a yoga teacher has always turned the proverbial mirror back towards me. If students are doing something that I don't like in class like showing up late or leaving early or following their own routine, I sit and ask myself why I am annoyed with this. And in fact learn something about myself. When I find that my teaching and sequences have gotten a bit stale, I return to more classes as a student to once again experience that side of the relationship so that I may tweak my approach when I return to being the teacher. There must always be a balance in the relationship. A swinging of the pendulum.

So I don't particularly think too much of myself as a teacher. I know that I have some knowledge available to me that I can share with the students who wish to receive it, but I know who I am. I'm not enlightened or evolved or anything like that. I've never shared revelations or moments of satori that I've had with my classes. (Saved those all for you!) Those are personal moments and not only that, but anytime you try to explain your moments of enlightenment, the words get all jumbled up and you come off speaking like you're just wrapping up a three day acid trip. Instead you try to share some struggles with them. In practice, in life, whatever. Making sure that while for the next hour or so I'm going to take on a specific role, but realize that it's just a hat that I'll be wearing for a moment, not a lifetime achievement award. I've always found that my least favorite part of class is the very beginning. I hate making eye contact and explaining what we are about to get into. It's difficult because you don't know everyone's reasons for being there. Once class starts and I'm in the act, I'm fine. The closing is easy too because by then I feel very comfortable in my hat. I've been wearing it for at least an hour and I've got it sitting on my head just right. But damn if the beginning isn't a little weird.

My power dynamic as far as the class is concerned is a switch that I turn on and off. I do try to consider what the student might be seeing though. If in a post class discussion it seems like I'm up on a pedestal for somebody, well maybe that's not the right person to grab a drink with. But the student who speaks to me about their connection to my struggles and the things that I've shared in class, that seems a little more available to explore. And as I said, these relationships and interactions can be generally frowned upon within the more 'purist' members of the yoga community. There's nothing wrong with that manner of thinking either. For them. If a teacher holds themselves to a certain standard and truly believes that they are in a place of power over their students, then they definitely shouldn't be fraternizing with them. But again it's their choice and how they want to run their class and their practice. The same decision could not be made for me and I don't think that I should be judged for it.

Because there's more to it here on my side too. I crave love and connection. The times when I've been in healthy committed relationships have been spectacular and I'd like to think that I will find one again, but this time even better than the past ones I've been in. Something so good that I don't even know that level of goodness yet. Something that I can't even fathom. And for a guy like me who is *kinda* spiritual, has a dedicated yoga practice, meditates regularly and writes whole *friggin* books on the internal work that occupies most of his time, where the hell do you think I might find a partner who has similar values and practices? Cause it sure as shit ain't at the bar. I'll tell you that much because I've looked.

Anytime I meet a woman at one of your classic LA bars on the Westside, it feels dirty. Like we both went to this one spot looking for love. We dressed a certain way and presented ourselves as a certain version to impress somebody in the same way that you'd present yourself positively in a job interview. You're appearing to be what you believe the person interviewing you might want to see. It's not a lie but it's not exactly the truth either now is it?

I contend that I'd rather see someone's struggles. I'd rather see someone who comes into my class after a rough week of work, muscles through the program and then lays in *savasana* for an extra twenty minutes to work that shit out on her own. I'd rather see someone who attempts the more difficult poses that we take in my class because she is unafraid and willing to push herself to her limits. I'd rather see someone that rain or shine no matter what they show up to my 6 AM Tuesday morning class because they are dedicated to self-improvement and a practice that isn't always easy. All of these are things that I value in myself and would surely value in a partner. I don't see those when I'm three deep at a bar on a Friday night. I may have some fleeting moments of love depending on what I'm imbibing but it all seems so contrived and forced. I like the love stories that happen by accident. The couple that met because they bumped into each other somewhere during their regular day. I like when it's not forced.

And yoga has never felt forced for me. The way I approach my yoga practice is not as a workout. I've gone to classes where I get a workout and I do love them, but it's not what yoga means to me. I have better ways of working out. But yoga has always been a meditative connection to my body. It's a space where I bridge the gap between what I want to do, what I think I'm capable of and the reality of where my body is at each moment in time. I can be working on inversions or more difficult postures but if I show up to class and my body doesn't have it on that day, I listen. It's not a no pain, no gain situation at all. It's a practice of listening to my body so that body and mind can get on the same page both on the mat and off of it. Yoga is a constant mirror so that I can see all the bullshit that I may be telling myself. It's a big fucking truth bomb every time. And it's a way in which I learn to love myself as I am.

Over the years I've become much closer with the dude from the trail. I tell everyone that I meet who knows him that he is one of my favorite people of all time. The reason I'm such a big supporter of his is because he is unapologetically himself at every moment of every day. He has some views and ideas that don't exactly vibe in the circles we run in. But he doesn't care. He's open about the way he feels and the way he lives his life. Our yoga is very different in a lot of ways. If you took his class and then mine I think you might even be surprised that we've taught at the same studios. But in a lot of ways, it's the same. It's a true moment not only for our students but for ourselves.

We certainly get to different truths. We don't agree on everything and we probably never will. But that's ok. We don't have to. His truth is not mine and my truth is not his. But we are both on the route to discover exactly what our truth is. And trying our best to live it. So even if the rest of the yoga community might think that we're breaking some unwritten law or code of conduct, that's fine with us. We've taken the good hard look at how we act and we sleep easy knowing that these values are our own. We decided on them.

Chapter 13

A QUICK WORD ABOUT LUCK

I used to play on a soccer team with a kid named Rafael. We called him Raf for short. This was my travel soccer team, so everybody on the squad was supposed to be able to play. It was quite a bit different from the team I had been on with my friends since we were four. This was more serious. I still remember Raf for several reasons. One of those reasons is that Raf tended to score a lot of goals for us. He wasn't our top scorer or our top player, but at the end of every season, he had quietly put a few in the back of the net that seemed to go unnoticed.

The other thing that I remember about Raf is that there wasn't anything particularly great about him as a player. That's not to say that he wasn't good or didn't have talent. There just wasn't anything that stood out to me at an age where I was sizing up guys left and right to try and get some sort of advantage. He wasn't the fastest guy on the team, but he could run. He didn't have the strongest shot, but he could always put something on it. His touches were okay and his defense was adequate. He could play the ball in the air, but you could just as easily muscle him off of it if you wanted to. When we split the team in half to scrimmage, I'd never be worried about him if he was on the other team, but I was always more than happy to have him line up on mine.

In those days, my dad and I used to break down games on the way home. We would meticulously go over the plays that went well and the ones that could have gone better. We'd also talk about the other players on the field as a way for me to learn how to better exist within the flow of the game, accentuating my teammates' stronger points and taking advantage of my opponent's weaknesses. This was all before I found Zen. This was back when I was a killer. I don't remember exactly when it happened but I do remember a conversation in the car about Raf. Raf's goals were rarely assisted. He wasn't a guy I typically looked out for or tried to get involved from my position at center mid, but he still tallied up goals. It was usually on a loose ball, errant cross, or something of that nature. Just Raf being in the right place at the right time. I thought that he was pretty lucky to score all those goals. But ever the student of the game, my dad thought there might be more to it than dumb luck.

Luck is an interesting concept that I play with in my own practice. There's not much thought given to it in the spiritual and religious texts that I've read. I guess the closest thing is the misunderstood idea of karma in the West that what goes around comes around, but I don't even think that really sums up what we think of as luck.

One way we tend to look at luck is through the use of luck charms. We decorate ourselves with little trinkets, like a penny from a grandfather or a bracelet made in Hawaii. We attach our own meanings to these lifeless totems and commit to the idea that they will bring us the things that we most desire. I, for one, dig the idea that you can implant energy into an object and carry it with you for some sort of protection. If you find something to be valuable, then it's valuable. No one can tell you otherwise.

We can also go a step further (and in Los Angeles, many people do). There is a great crystal culture out here, as I'm sure there is in many other parts of the world, and it can get pretty crazy. The same rock that I bought for fifteen dollars not ten minutes outside of Zion National Park in Utah can go for eighty dollars in Venice. The scene is so intense that Mystic Journey, a famous mystical bookstore and crystal shop on Abbot Kinney, opened up a second location strictly for viewing larger crystal pieces on Lincoln Boulevard. In both shops, you can buy the crystal bible, a full-on anthology of each crystal type including what they mean and what they do.

My favorite crystal is hematite. Hematite is a dark and dense crystal that looks like some type of stainless steel when polished. I'm always amazed at the weight and density of the stone. It reminds me of one of the opening scenes in *Lord of the Rings* when Gandalf drops the One Ring into Frodo's hand. As Frodo catches it, his hand recoils downward at the weight of it. For something so little, it carries a surprising weight. This is further amplified later in the first movie when Boromir tells Frodo that he carries the weight of us all. But let's hop back before I go down the Tolkien rabbit hole. Hematite is a stone that is used specifically for grounding. It is said to help the wearer or holder keep their own energy without taking on any energy from the people or things that surround them. In other words, the wearer is un-phased by anything outside themselves.

I started my adult career as an orthopedic physical therapist working in a clinic where I could see twenty to thirty patients a day in a ten-hour shift. Each and every person came in with some type of physical ailment or complaint and it was my job to figure out what was going on and set them on the path to recovery. I had a professor in college who told me that the biggest hurdle that I personally would run into as a physical therapist was that people weren't cars. I had a good understanding of anatomy and kinesiology, so I knew how everything was supposed to work within the body. What I lacked at the time was empathy toward my patients and what they were going through. I would sit across from them, asking what was going on with their body, and

then I would basically zone out as they told me what I saw as inconsequential details to the diagnosis. I didn't want to deal with the mom who "didn't have time" to do her home exercise program because she was running a household. From my point of view, it was very simple. If you wanted to get better, you do your exercises. If you didn't do your exercises, that was like going to your doc and then deciding not to take the medication that he prescribed.

When I moved to California, I had a bit more time to spend with my patients. Not much, but enough that I started to notice some trends. I began to see groups of patients. There were the athletes who couldn't be bothered with what I was saying. They just wanted me to fix them. There were the intellectuals who wanted to understand what was going on, but didn't really want to put in any of the hard work to get better. There were the lonely older people who wanted me to feel bad for them and show them sympathy. The last group I had no time for. That wasn't my job. I had gone to school to learn about the body and how to treat it. If my patients needed someone to hold their hand and tell them that it was all going to be alright, well that just wasn't me. I chalked it up as the patients who wanted to get better would and the ones who wanted to complain, well, they could complain to my aides. I didn't want to hear it.

And that was one of my biggest problems. I just didn't want to hear it. It was so incredibly draining to have patient after patient walk into my clinic complaining about this or that. Even though it was my job, it all felt like whining to me. I took on so much negative energy and was completely shot by the end of each day. I found myself to be irritable and easily annoyed and I didn't have the energy to take care of myself after a day of taking care of everyone else. I had effectively taken on everyone else's pain and struggles into my own body.

This is where my hematite comes in. As we discussed earlier, hematite is a fairly dense crystal. It pulls you back down into the physical if you're getting all up into your headspace. It grounds you into your own space as others try to drag you into theirs. I was taking the job home with me. There was a certain sense of responsibility I had for my patients. I had to struggle with the same challenges they were on a daily basis if I was going to be able to put them on the path to recovery. Looking back, it all seems so terribly vain of me to think that I could actually cure or fix someone. I've since learned that I'm only a guide. It's the patient or the client that does all the work and I can only point them in the right direction. It does neither of us any good for me to take on their pain or struggle. No one can pour from an empty cup.

So as a healer attempting to take care of myself first, I started sporting some hematite jewelry. It began with a hematite mala necklace that was gifted to me by my partner. I don't wear it all the time anymore as I think I have a better handle on my energies, but use it if I know at the beginning of the day that I'll be going down some darker roads with more difficult patients. It's a reminder to me that what is theirs is theirs and that I'm grounded in my own energy no matter what comes up at work.

At this time, I started getting questions from my friends back home about this new jeweled-up style. I'm not embarrassed or anything like that, but it's taking a bit of a risk telling my friends that I'm wearing a necklace to energetically ground myself. If you disclose this, you're going to get ripped a bit, as you should, by the way. The way I worked around some of this was by admitting that I didn't know if a stone that I held in my pocket or a bracelet I wore on my wrist was really having a dramatic effect on the energy of my day. Maybe it was. There was no real way of disproving it, but then again, I wouldn't stake my reputation on it. However, I would say that my morning ritual of taking a stone and bracelet off of my altar and putting them on my body with the same regularity that I was brushing my teeth could certainly have an effect. I was approaching my day with intention. The intention that I set was to be grounded in my personal space and to not take on the energy of the injured and sick people that I would come into contact with daily. I made it a point to wear them because they protected me. But maybe the thought or reminder that I needed a little bit of protection was enough to remind me to protect myself. No stone was necessary.

As I began exploring the energy of different stones and crystals, I was introduced to the wonders of reiki energy healing. When I first found this healing art, I was even more skeptical of it than I was of stones. How could you heal someone without touching them? It seemed hippie-dippy, even for my taste. But the woman who first began speaking to me about reiki was someone that I trusted more than the art itself. She just seemed to hold herself to a high energetic standard. I distrust people who are happy all the time or live by the phrase "good vibes only." Those are the people who can't seem to operate in the real world. However, I had met this woman several times and was starting to see that it wasn't an act. It was who she truly was. Much like the male yoga teacher I discussed earlier, she was just someone who seemed right out of a hippie stereotype and I didn't trust it. Until I spent time with her and realized that this was one hundred percent authentic.

At a time when I started to feel my energy fading from all of the work that I was doing on patients, she posted on her account letting her followers know that she would be attuning those who wanted to embark on their reiki journey. Attunement is basically the wording used for going through a teacher training and getting a certification to perform reiki healing. I'm typically terrible at making decisions, but I'm also very comfortable sitting and listening. In times where I can get very quiet and allow my ego to drop back for a minute, the universe does tend to speak very clearly to me. This was one of those times. So I signed up and was attuned.

Over the course of the next two days, I learned a lot about reiki. I'll spare you the details, but I really did walk away with quite a few tools that I could use to prevent myself from taking on someone else's energy. There was a visualization that I could incorporate prior to seeing the patient and then a post-session routine that I could do to make sure I "cleansed" myself after the session.

Who knows if envisioning myself in a tube of clear white energy before going into a patient's session and then swiping energy off of my arms and throwing it away post-session actually does anything in the physical world. I really don't know. And to be honest, if there was a study on the subject, I wouldn't be interested in reading it. It's not something that can be tested. What I will say is that I was taking precautions before I entered to remind myself that what's mine is mine and what's theirs is theirs. In the end, I was taking a moment to remind myself that whatever had just happened no longer had to have any effect on my day. It was done and that was that.

I would have never thought I'd be the guy to talk to about crystals and reiki. It seems so far removed from what I typically think. But what's the difference between a lucky rabbit's foot in one pocket and a hematite stone in the other? Who can separate the elaborate routines baseball players go through before stepping into the batter's box and some pre-session movements I do? To me, it all seems like intention setting. Taking a moment to decide how you want to approach the upcoming situation before you jump headfirst into it. Aristotle was known for saying, "We are what we repeatedly do. Excellence, then, is not an act, but a habit." Maybe the same could be said of being lucky.

By eighth grade, I had left my travel soccer team in favor of football. I couldn't play both sports in the fall season. By winter, I had turned to basketball. One evening, my dad and I made our way to the CYO center in Port Richmond to play St. Joseph Hill's team. I didn't think about much going into the game. They weren't one of our rivals and I don't remember them being that good. I couldn't even picture anyone from their team, which is weird for me even now as I can recall the good players from each and every school on the Island. But we showed up and there was Raf, lining up across from me for the start of the game. We hadn't seen each other since I left the team, so we said hi but then quickly got lost in the spirit of competition and the flow of the game.

I don't remember the final score or the box score or any really specific details of the game, but I do remember Raf. I remember him scoring on rebound put backs, getting easy steals on bad passes, and just generally being in the right place at the right time to capitalize on the situation. If I hadn't known him before the game, I never would have noticed those things. I would have just written him off as a decent kid on the other team getting lucky a few times throughout the game. But that was Raf. He was always in the right place at the right time. That was his thing. Maybe he kept some sort of stone in his pocket that got him there. Maybe he had a whole pregame ritual that prepared him to compete. Or maybe he made his own luck with his own intentions.

Hard to say, really.

Chapter 14

GHOSTS, SPIRITS, AND OTHER THINGS I'M NOT SURE I BELIEVE IN

A yoga class can be an interesting thing. I tend to find that it's very rarely about the yoga. Any class I've ever hated could be attributed back to something outside of the class that I was feeling. Teachers that I've loved have been amazing when I first met them and then terrible once I got to know them as actual people off their mats. It's all me. It has nothing to do with them.

Sometimes, I like to go into yoga a little self-medicated. I'm not a huge supporter of all the mind-expanding drugs and stimulants you can ingest. I'm not against them, either. I think that everyone has to make that choice for themselves because I've seen people bloom into their truest selves while tripping their face-off and I've seen people travel to their deepest, darkest hells. Both can teach you something and then from there, you can decide if you should continue down that path or not. It's just important to own the decision.

One day in early spring, I had some clients cancel on me, creating a nice little half-day. As I wrapped up a session in the valley, I could feel the sun getting warmer and was convinced that the best way to spend the extra time was to go to the beach.

I raced home on the 405 and quickly packed a bag with a blanket, towel, some White Claws Hard Seltzer, a joint, and a book. When I got down to the beach just south of the Santa Monica Pier, it became very apparent that it was not a beach day. My shirt never even came off. I just sat there bundled up in my hoodie, drinking my Claws and trying to read my book. Needless to say, the beach trip was cut much shorter than I had originally planned. I got back home and was feeling a little wavy (one of my favorite ways to feel) and I realized that I could scooter over to my studio to take a class with a teacher that I had a little yoga crush on. So I boogied across Wilshire to the studio on San Vicente and said my hellos with no one the wiser and took a spot in the back of the class.

Everyone has their own reasons for drinking or doing drugs or really anything that they do. I find that when I step into my altered states, I can get out of my own way. I don't neurotically turn over each and every point of the decision that I'm making. I just make the decision. So in this class, the ego was on thin ice and as the teacher stepped onto her mat to introduce herself, I was hit with a very distinct urge to take the class with my eyes closed. I don't usually do this. I even tend to meditate with my eyes open to keep all the senses present. But again, I didn't question the urge. I just decided to lean into it.

Taking class with your eyes closed is interesting. You're constantly feeling for the edges of your mat to make sure you haven't veered to a 45-degree angle half facing the student next to you. It really wouldn't matter if you did, but I like to honor the space of others in the room and be as little of a potential disruption to their practice as I can be. Your balance also sucks with your eyes closed. Balance is made up of your proprioception, your vestibular system, and your vision. So if you take away vision, everything has to work a lot harder to keep you upright. Both of these bring a little more focus to your practice and you can't really drift off into the different thoughts that stumble through your mind on a regular basis.

The studio where I teach has specific things that they like you to do while teaching. One of the things that they encourage and that I feel incredibly uncomfortable with is addressing students by name. This is supposed to bring a sense of teacher-student relationship, showing that you see them as individuals and you are trying to help them, not just the class. I do a ton of hands-on assists when I teach, so I've never felt the need to do this. But I'm also bad with names, so maybe I'm just defending myself. I'm sure it's a bit of both.

Anyway, I'm rolling through my first sun salutation, really just tuning into my body and the vibrations that come about with just a little bit of alcohol in the system, and the teacher says, "Great job, Kristy."

Kristy is the name we'll use for the former partner of mine who I mentioned earlier. As you can imagine with it coming up occasionally in this book, I've had a lot to process after that relationship ended. It's a wound that will never fully heal. I'm embarrassed to still write about it, but I've come to terms with the scar. I'd rather address the scar when I notice it than try to hide it.

So I hear the name Kristy, and it travels right up my spine and hits me in the middle of the heart chakra. And I don't mean that as a metaphor. The vibrational sound of that name affected me. I didn't open my eyes. I knew she wasn't there. She wouldn't be caught dead at this studio (hipster). I shook the feeling off and got back into my practice

Moments later, I was right where I had left off, laser-focused on what I was doing so that I wouldn't fall over and look like an ass. I had pretty much forgotten about my teacher's cues until she said it again!

I heard the name again and I could feel it right in the middle of my chest, the way it feels when you're heartbroken and you have literal pain at the heart. I started to think the same way that I thought when I first heard the name. Shake it off. Ignore it. Keep your focus.

Then I questioned that response.

Why not lean into it? This was coming up for a reason. Let it happen and see where it takes you.

I let my heart ache a little bit and didn't try to fix it, but let that pain wash over me. It was like getting a tattoo. You can't fight the pain. It's happening and it's not going to end for quite some time. So make peace with it, and you will be better for the decision. As I leaned into this feeling, I got a distinct feeling of a presence from the direction where I had heard her name. I continued to move in the practice and while I can't say that I saw her, I could feel her in a very visual sense. I could "see" a premonition start to dance over in the corner of the room far away from me. She flowed effortlessly with the music. She always did. She was one of those beautiful yoga goddesses who knew the ins and outs and curves of her body so well that to see her in movement was to see her at her best. Up on her tiptoes, she twirled around the room, swaying her hands through the air and leaving little ghostly waves in her wake.

She took her time moving toward me. I kept thinking she was coming to me, then she would turn the other direction as if she knew I was there but was unconcerned with this knowledge. She might end up in my area or she might not. It didn't matter to her.

All the while, I got deeper into my practice, bringing all of my focus to a toe stand so that I wouldn't fall. I was trying to impress her, I'll admit it. But she didn't notice. She just continued to dance as if she was the only one in the room.

Her teasing got closer and closer to me. I reached forward before dropping into an extended side angle pose and I swear that she moved just out of the grasp of my upper arm. When I arched backward into a reverse warrior, I could feel her hand close to my heart as I created some space and begged for that touch. Each time I stretched my body in one direction, she would lean the other like it was some invisible energy tango. We used to dance like this. Getting closer and closer but not touching. Just teasing.

Class began to slow down, as it always does, and she began to fade away. I could barely feel her as I went through the motions of the more restorative postures in sitting and on my back. I twisted each way and she was not there. I went into happy baby and she was not there. I curled up into a ball and I felt nothing.

Then I hit *savasana*, my final resting place.

I spread out into a starfish laying on my back. And she returned.

I could feel her curl up into that tiny ball laying on her side and facing me. She was right underneath my arm nuzzling herself into my embrace like the little kitten that she was. And we laid through most of the *savasana* like that, in the embrace that I had missed for so long. Mere moments before the teacher roused us from our sleep to close out class, she brought her face very close to mine. She leaned in and whispered in my ear.

"Let go of your burden."

Then she was gone. The presence, the essence, the spirit had completely vanished. Many students and other teachers have told me about their experiences crying in class and that rarely, if ever, happens to me. But I was pretty damn close here. I laid in the darkroom for quite some time. Long after every other student had packed up their things and left, I was still there. It was the manager of the studio who came into the room and roused me before the training staff could come in. Right away, she knew I had experienced something in that class. It's usually one class out of a hundred that hits you in a certain way, but that's why we do the practice.

Most religions believe in some sort of otherworldly being that lives within our existence but is just outside of our walls of perception. These beings only interact with the spiritually devout or the utterly insane. Some call them spirits, some call them ghosts, some call them angels. I'm not sure what to call it, but I'm pretty sure it's something

That class was different. It was very different from the regular class that I take every Tuesday at 7:30 AM where I work on my breathing and different postures. That was a class I had no thought of taking until I stepped into the universal flow, sometimes called the Tao. I had a certain idea for how my day would go and then something came up. Rather than fight against it or pout about my bad luck, I gave it some space and another idea appeared into my mind. I felt a pull to go to yoga. And I find it a little more than coincidental that in a class I just happened to get the urge to go take, I had such a deep and profound experience. Say that I was drunk. Go ahead, I don't care. Because I had definitely been in my cups. But I was also functional enough to complete an entire class with my eyes closed. So, maybe the alteration to my regular state could actually be helpful and something that I can work with rather than just use to blame my mistakes on. Fuck that. A little booze in the system allows you to act without caring. It helps you get out of your own way. It allowed me, in this instance, to actually believe the abnormal feelings that I had of a presence that I had not felt in a very, very long time.

I don't believe in reincarnation in the sense that this version of my body will appear in a different body at some point in the universe. I don't believe in an afterlife where this version of myself will continue to live in some sort of heaven or hell. What I do believe in is energy. The molecules that make up my body are constantly changing. I'm not the same bundle of atoms today that I was last year, last month, or even yesterday. But that energy has to go somewhere, so maybe sometimes little pieces of energy that used to exist in the person you knew or the place you lived get back together in your vicinity and give you that feeling you remember. That nostalgia or angel-like presence. I'm not entirely sure that I believe that, but I can't disprove it either. So I guess you could say I'm open to the idea. And that feels like a really good place to be.

Chapter 15

THE STUPID AND INSIGHTFUL THINGS SAID IN A YOGA STUDIO

At this point in our saga, you've probably realized that I have a bit of a love-hate relationship with myself as a yoga teacher. On one hand, I love that yoga has given me a mindful way to connect with my body and the ability to teach and share the connection with people around me. On the other hand, there's some really non-yogic shit that goes on in the yoga community these days and probably always. It's just the nature of the beast, I guess.

There are a lot of things that I love about teaching at CorePower Yoga. To start, I get paid. You can say all you want about taking yoga and turning it into some sort of corporate enterprise, but my paycheck is on-time and my classes are regularly scheduled. When you've taught at a number of mom-and-pop studios where you may get paid late or sometimes not at all and classes may be moved or cancelled due to the owner's interest in the newest female teacher, well... you tend to appreciate structure. I also can vibe with the way that they teach the practice, to a certain degree. When I started teaching, I was all about the physical side of the practice and CorePower Yoga happened to be a studio that centered on that. Mind you, there's nothing wrong with a more flowery, existential approach, but the physical workout class is a great way to get people like me in the door, at least in the beginning. I was once in a study about men in yoga and the researcher told me that almost every single one of the male yoga teachers she spoke with first found the practice by following a woman there. So we don't all come to the mat seeking spiritual salvation or with the proper intentions, but in the end I don't think that really matters. The practice becomes what you need it to be.

There are also things that I don't like there. One of the things I tend to rebel against is the language and structure they want us to teach our classes. In training, they teach instructors to say things like, "Move *your* knee over *your* ankle" or "Raise *your* hands over *your* head." I lean toward using "*the* knee" and "*the* head." When my teachers brought this to my attention, I got into a long monologue about how there is no ownership over the body part and no need to use a possessive pronoun. We couldn't really say who owned the knee, so referring to it as *the* knee probably made more sense... Okay, so maybe I was being a bit of a dick there, but by this point you know that I'm all for questioning authority.

However, something that really twisted me up inside at CorePower was something that I refer to as "the thing." One manager I worked under who knew me fairly well would recommend classes I might like, but would also warn me that this teacher was going to do "the thing." I'd sigh, roll my eyes, and step into the class anyway. Now "the thing" is this: Teachers in core power training are taught to connect with their students, so a new teacher (and some of the older ones who haven't shaken off this incredibly weird and awkward practice) will open up class by taking their position at the front of the class, kneeling on the mat, and saying something like this:

"Hey guys! I'm Rainbow. Welcome to class. This week I've just been dealing with a lot. I wasn't able to get my usual parking space at work and my dog pooped inside twice this week so I think he's getting really sick and I'm worried. Then today I finally had my breaking point when they spelled my name wrong on my almond milk latte. And I've just been feeling like the whole world is resting on my shoulders and I'm just really, really... (pause for effect) struggling, ya know!? But last night I took a nice warm bath with

lavender soap and had a glass of wine and really treated myself and realized that it's alright and I'm actually super lucky. So I just want to remind you in this class to take care of yourself and remember how lucky you really are, okay!? Child's pose!"

Shoot me.

Obviously, I embellished a little bit here but you get the idea. CorePower teaches a form of yoga that appeals to middle to upper class clientele. From that pool of students, they train teachers. They train those teachers to connect with their students and their struggles. And believe me, everybody struggles. I know this. You could grow up in utter poverty or you could be Elon Musk's son with the impossible name and you'll still run into struggles and issues throughout your life. When something comes up, they encourage the teachers to share it. It brings them closer to their students and puts everyone on the same level. But let's not reach. Let's not share for the sake of sharing and rack our brains for what is bothering us at the current moment. You don't always *need* a story. You don't always *need* to be working on something. This sort of storytelling in the yoga and spiritual communities leads to something that I see a lot of these days.

Victimization.

Let's preface a lot of what I'm about to say with some facts so they don't lock me up and throw away the key when this book comes out. First, I'm a white, relatively straight male. As far as the privilege lottery goes, I pretty much hit the jackpot. And I say "relatively straight" not to hide my sexuality, but to recognize that my experience in that arena is not the same as it is for a gay individual in this world. I'd also like to acknowledge that there are many people in this world who have gone through things that no one should have to go through. Extreme poverty, emotional and physical abuse, rape... I mean the list goes on and on. I don't think it's fair to paint with such a broad brushstroke so it seems like I'm saying that anyone and everyone who has ever shared their own struggles is playing the role of whiney victim. That's not what I'm saying at all.

I do, however, think that the human consciousness loves these stories. We love the stories of insurmountable odds and the heroes who defied them. In one of the most quoted pieces from Tolkien, Sam tells Frodo, "It's like in the great stories, Mr. Frodo. The ones that really mattered. Full of darkness and danger, they were. And sometimes you didn't want to know the ending. Because how could the ending be happy? How could the world go back to the way it was when so much bad had happened? But in the end, it's only a passing thing, this shadow. Even darkness must pass. A new day will come. And when the sun shines it will shine out clearer. Those are the stories that stayed with you. That meant something, even if you were too small to understand why. But I think, Mr. Frodo, I do understand. I know now. Folk in those stories had lots of chances to turn back, only they didn't. They kept going."

If you're a *Lord of the Rings* fan, you've probably heard the joke surrounding the epic saga that they should have just ridden the eagles to Mordor and dropped the ring in the volcano. It would've saved thousands of lives, miles of journey, and shortened three never-ending movies into one thirty-minute episode. But that's not a story. That's not an epic to rival *Star Wars*. No, to make a story, you need some conflict. You need a tale of heroics and daring. A moment where you know that your hero is surrounded by danger on all sides and, as things look their bleakest and there seems to be no way that he could possibly succeed, he slithers through a crack, that one in a million chance, and wins the day. That's the story that inspires you to do better, to be better. Because anything is possible.

We all grew up watching or reading stories like this. Maybe you're not a Tolkien fan, (I'll take the moment to let you know that this is your opinion which you are entitled to, but also that your opinion is wrong) but I'm sure you can pick out another story from your youth that follows the classic hero archetype. I believe these stories to be good things. I believe that it's important to know the unstoppable human spirit and the limitless potential that each of us has.

What I don't believe in is backtracking your story. When you're in it, what you are going through is important. It's the most important thing at the moment because as we have already explored, there probably only is this moment. Past and future are merely concepts that we can't actually visit. So when you're in it and you're really going through it, then leaning on your Luke Skywalkers and Jon Snows for inspiration is amazing. It's gotten me through some long runs that I certainly didn't want to finish. Hey, if Jon Snow can climb the wall, I can run eighteen miles, right? For me, backtracking is taking where you're at now, looking at the roadblocks and obstacles that you had to overcome to get where you're at, and then embellishing them to create a story of greater renown.

We all want to be Jon Snow. We all believe that we are the center of the universe and the one who can and will save the world. But really, it's much more likely that we are soldier number three in the Battle of the Bastards who are taken out by a random arrow shot into the mix. Don't believe me? Let's do a little math. I live in Los Angeles, a city that at the time I'm writing this estimates a population of about four million people. Out of those four million, I'd be surprised to know if more than 500 people in the city knew who I actually was. And 500 is being fairly generous, I think. So maybe the circle that I actively affect is 500 out of a possible 4 million in my city. And that's just the city. Expand to the supposed population of California at 39.51 million and my reach and impact shrink exponentially. Expand again to the population of the United States at 328.2 million and then the world at 7 billion. My 500 is measly. Puny even. So while these stories are effective in inspiring me to be a little bit better each day, let's have a little chaser to the thought of how important we might be.

This might be a sobering thought. Some may even say it's a depressing thought. I tend to disagree quite firmly. People in positions of power have this burden of affecting and changing thousands to millions of lives that they will never meet. They can conceptualize the numbers, but they can never know one Frank from the thousands of others. Their decisions are all made on conceptualization. My ideas don't have to be like that. Within my circle of the estimated 500, I can see each individual and I can act in accordance with what might be the best action at the moment. The powerful cannot, as they know that caving to that one person's best interests may be detrimental to the rest of the people they are responsible for. It's a conundrum, for sure. One that I am not jealous of in the slightest.

We got a little off track there, but we're about to come back around. The point, which I took the scenic route to make, is that you don't have to be the hero of the story to have a positive or negative effect on the people around you. You can have a positive effect on someone who's not even in your circle by holding the door open or sharing a smile. It's really that simple.

I think, however, that marketing yourself as the overcomer of obstacles and the one true hero of the story is all too common within the yoga community. And it is a competitive one. Who wouldn't want to make their living by teaching what could be described as a peaceful yet energizing fitness class for your body and mind? It sounds like a pretty good gig. It just doesn't pay well. So in order to make that dream of being a fulltime yoga instructor a reality, you've got to hustle and convince other people why they should commit to your practice rather than the hundreds of other yoga teachers in the greater Los Angeles area.

We sometimes do this by creating a story of how we were once lost and now are found through the great practice of yoga. In marketing, you are taught to first create your potential buyers' hell to empathize with them. To show them that you know all too well where they are right now. From there, you can let them know how you faced the same struggles, persevered, and survived to emerge at the top of the mountain as a new, enlightened, and glorious being. You've taken them on a journey through the mind and now they want to do what you've done. But there are quite a few problems with this route. First off, you ain't perfect. You're also not enlightened. How do I know? Because enlightened isn't something you become. It's something you experience once in a while. Looking at it as a summit you achieve and stay on top of is just plain wrong. You also have now built up a story for yourself as a teacher that you have to keep going back to.

Maybe you really did go through some tough times and unimaginable pain, grief, and sorrow. It's possible you persevered with a severely dysfunctional family or in an abusive relationship. Maybe you have had poor self-worth, body image, or eating disorders. If you feel like you're in a space where you've gotten through those dark times, wouldn't it be incredibly triggering and difficult to have to constantly return to those spaces? Wouldn't you begin to live in that story instead of wrapping it up, signing off, and closing the book? I often find myself feeling empathetic and sad for musicians who write a great song about heartbreak or despair. I can't imagine having to go back and play the song that I ripped out of my chest and bled onto the page for every single show. It would be reliving the pain all over again. It's hard to grow if you keep digging into the soil again and again and again.

This is why I find some things said in and around the yoga studio to be frustrating or counter-productive to the actual practice. Identification with a story when the goal of the practice is to detach from ego and become the experience is as oxymoronic as it gets. So, yes, I've been triggered by the yoga studio and I want to explore a few more things that I've heard that knot me up like a cartoon character when I hear them. But as we discuss my initial reactions, stick with me, because there is always something to be learned. There are no good teachers and no bad teachers, simply experience as the best possible teacher.

One such insult to my ill-conceived notion of what yoga should or shouldn't be came from my time teaching at a little studio called Create Yoga. The studio lasted less than a year but was one of my favorite places of all time. I had a Sunday 9:30 AM class that was regularly around twenty people. I found it to be a church. The studio was beautiful. The owners were dedicated to their employee's satisfaction, going so far as to, in my opinion, egregiously overpay us. Due to some unavoidable, and possibly some avoidable, circumstances the studio was forced to shut down.

I had one woman in my class regularly who had a strong practice. She wasn't flipping upside down and touching her toes to her forehead or anything like that, but you could see that she heard the cues I was giving and adjusted her practice accordingly. She'd also stay after class and ask me about certain poses and movements. You could tell that she was there to learn. One day after class, she waited for the other students to shuffle out of the lobby so that she could ask me a question. She told me that she was having this weird nerve sensation going down her left leg. It seemed like it started at her glute and traveled down the outside of her leg all the way to her ankle and sometimes even into her foot. I began to ask her questions about which poses caused the sensation to grow and which poses caused it to subside, if and when she felt it off of her mat, how long it had been going on for, etc. Just the usual physical therapy questions that I would ask in any regular evaluation. The woman who used to work at the front desk during my class is an incredible yoga teacher. She's a retired professional athlete who spent time as a competitive dancer and even in the lingerie football league. Her yoga is nothing short of amazing. There's no pose that she can't do. Well, she overhead our little pow-wow and offered up her two cents on the subject.

"Is there a woman with negative energy in your life?" she asked.

I think I spit out the coffee that I wasn't drinking when I heard that. I mean, what the fuck? First off, everyone has a woman in their life with negative energy. That's a non-question. Even if you love your mom to death, I'm sure she's still got some thoughts on how you could be doing better and I venture to guess that she's not shy about sharing them with you. Or maybe it's a girlfriend or partner who wants the best for you and pushes you in a certain direction. Or maybe it's a co-worker. Who knows? The point is, yes, we all have a woman with negative energy in our lives. Second, we're having a serious discussion here. I'm breaking down pelvic alignment, glute strength,

and hamstring flexibility. I'm twisting her body one way and the other to see if we are pinching on a nerve. I'm testing the sensation of different dermatomes spreading throughout the leg. I've got a goddamn medical degree. And she's asking about negative energies.

At the time, it all seemed stupid. It still *kinda* does. But I've also failed in my assessments and treatments of patients enough times to realize that the western medicine I was trained in does not have all of the answers. That's why we call it "practicing medicine." You don't know for sure what you're doing and you're going to make mistakes. We don't have all the answers and we never will. The problem is that somebody like me that has dedicated a lot of time and money into learning this western medicine has a lot to lose if it's not respected. So to disprove it or poke holes in the thought process can really put my livelihood and profession on shaky ground. My first thought is to pump my chest up a bit when someone takes a different perspective on medical issues. Stay in your own lane! But it's important to consider the fact that you might be wrong. And if someone gives you another way of thinking that could shed some light on your problem, then a thank you probably works better for your patient or clients or student. In the end, that's what we as medical providers all want, I hope.

Another teacher sent me into a similarly short-lived conniption on this topic. This was a teacher who I had met once or twice and had come highly recommended to me by my studio manager, but I had some reservations about it. To be fair, the manager did warn that she was a bit flowery for my taste, meaning that the class was less anatomically sound and may dive deeper into a hippie-dippie spiritual aspect. I was game to test-drive it though, so I made it a point to get to this class that was somewhat outside of my usual yoga schedule. I'm not entirely sure what was going on with me that day, but I do know that I came in a bit snippy. It wasn't five minutes in before she hit us with a line.

"Take the time now to close your eyes. They say that vision can be the most distracting of the senses."

I take full ownership of my mood going in, but that shit is stupid. In what way is vision the most distracting of the senses? I mean, try settling into a class and your zen zone as a car alarm blares outside. Try to reach enlightenment through the sacred practice as the dude next to you sweats out the Indian food he consumed twenty minutes before class and you try to not choke on the stench. All of the senses can be distracting. None more than the others. I could also ask who the "they" is who offered her that prophetic wisdom, but that's almost too easy of a target.

Let's look at why such a statement would trigger me so hard and launch me out of my safe space. For starters, the type of meditation that I practice most often involves keeping the eyes open. Rather than closing out distractions, you welcome them. You keep your eyes open and notice all of the things going on around you because there are always things going on around you. You don't try to stop them or block them out or create a magical utopia in your mind but instead, you sit with the reality of the situation, no matter what that reality is. I associate this distinction as the difference between finding peace whilst sitting on a beach with warm breezes and blue skies versus trying to find that same peace on a rainy Tuesday morning when you're late for work. One without the other isn't that useful to me. We can all be nice and Zen-sitting on a beach. We just can't stay on the beach forever.

The other half of the statement is the delivery in which it was given. This teacher had a vibe that I'm usually not too on board for. It was more of a worldly deal with types of music she was playing, a ton of Sanskrit being used, and, just like I was warned, an overall flowery disposition. It felt like a sales pitch. It felt like a corruption of what a yoga teacher should be as if she had read all about it and was now putting on a show starring the perfect yoga teacher. And then to say something like that, as if it had years and years of ancient lore attached to it, just felt like an entire crock of shit to me.

I left that class pissed off. I went home right away and wrote a whole article about keeping your eyes open during meditation. I put the whole class on blast. I didn't call her out personally or anything like that, and I hope that I don't make a habit of doing that, but I certainly tore apart that statement. Then an interesting thing happened. In the next class that I went to, with a teacher who I was admittedly crushing on at the time, I was hit with a strong desire to take the class with my eyes closed. The entire sixty minutes of class was in darkness. My balance postures were more difficult. I had to constantly use my hands to check where my mat was and to ensure that I was still facing forward. It wound up being an extremely challenging class for me. One that I was incredibly focused for. To some extent, I believe I may have been doing this so that I wouldn't find my eyes following the teacher around the room and give off my less than pure intentions. With my eyes closed, I would appear as the perfect yogi, dedicated to his practice.

And there it is!

Thus far, I've told a couple of little stories about me being uncomfortable with people in this community, regular students, and well-learned and traveled teachers alike. My first instinct seems to be to label people as hypocrites or being less than they say they are. In that way, I've got a little Holden Caulfield in me. If you have to look him up, go for it, but I know a high school English teacher who would be very disappointed in you. The person I know best in this world is myself. I know that I don't always have pure intentions. I know where my mind goes. I know what I do and what I've done and I know that not all of that would pass the holiness test. My assumption is that most people are the same. So I hear the person at the podium preaching over the masses and wonder what right they have to stand there.

That's the thing, though. A teacher doesn't have to be perfect. A teacher doesn't even have to be a good teacher. A bad teacher can teach you a lot of lessons if you choose to accept those lessons. In this case, this teacher had a lovely lesson to teach me. That the practice can change in fantastic ways. That you can see the practice through another's eyes if you hear them out on how they approach it and try it out for yourself. It doesn't mean that your initial approach was wrong or that theirs was right, but it can allow you to add to and develop your practice as you go. It's accepting the seat of a student and going out to search without any preconceived notion of what you might find. You can't pour more tea into a cup that is already full.

The main point of these two stories is just that: Yoga is a crazy little practice. So is Zen. So is Taoism. But by that definition, so is

Catholicism. So is Judaism. So is Islam. And the list will continue to get longer and longer if you want it to. The last time I was in a Catholic Church was for my best friend from grade school's wedding. They opted to have the full-length mass at their ceremony and let me tell you that some of the things we Catholics say in church are BANANAS!

The sacrament of the Eucharist is not considered to be a symbol in the faith of my Father. No, we believe that the cracker and wine we consume are *literally* the body and blood of Jesus Christ. That's Catholic dogma. And I know quite a few Catholics who wouldn't bat an eye at that assertion and yet find it pretty ridiculous to hear me ramble on about the chakras or energy and reiki. That is a full cup mindset. That is knowing the things that you know and believing that to be enough.

But it's never enough. The pursuit of knowledge of any kind is not one that ends. Socrates had the only true knowledge of the universe in knowing that he knew nothing. There was just simply too much going on for him to come to any definitive knowledge. That is why we can't walk into a class to learn with the mind of a teacher, as someone who is going to give feedback on the class or some other nonsense. That's not being a student. And in not being a student, we rob ourselves of our own ability to learn. Admittedly, it is very difficult for me to sit in the seat of a student. I've struggled with so many teachers along my path and I think I tend to do best with the ones that are far separated from me or that I don't see on a regular basis so that I don't have to feel that insecurity of not knowing enough in front of an actual person. But that's my shit. I still try to take those crazy things I hear in a yoga class and notice my reaction to them. I sit with that reaction and wonder why it played out the way that it did. And sometimes, when I think about it long and hard, that stupid thing actually becomes pretty damn enlightening. I just have to leave space for the lesson to unfold.

Chapter 16

I THINK I KINDA MIGHT BE LOSING IT A LITTLE BIT MAYBE

I mentioned author Jack Kerouac previously, and he is my favorite author of all time. As one of the famous authors of the beat generation, Kerouac committed himself to his unique form of Buddhism by writing in one stream of consciousness. Toward the end of his career, critics suggested that he was releasing whatever came to his mind in an attempt to make some money. But another famous poet and his friend, Allen Ginsberg, came to his defense, arguing that Kerouac's commitment to writing things exactly as they happened and attention to detail in his remembered events was something that literature had never seen before. Kerouac's final book, *Big Sur*, uses little to no punctuation and reads like a long run-on stream of thought coming from a troubled alcoholic's mind (which he was). He would later die of a massive hemorrhage.

This chapter might come off a bit odd, but this is my attempt at an open stream of consciousness and a peek into the Sméagol/ Gollum-like battle that exists within my mind on a regular basis. I may or may not have been self-medicating at the time of writing this. Enjoy.

I think a lot of people get into spirituality in search of happiness. It's a noble endeavor. I mean, who doesn't want to be happy? I think if you offered happiness to anybody, they would gladly take it. But

I don't think any of us really know or understand what happiness is, and we certainly don't understand how to go about obtaining it.

Happiness is like an idea. It's more of a puff of smoke than a tangible object. It's this little thing that shows up once in a while, but you never notice it when it's present and only remember it when it's gone. I like to think of singer/songwriters like Bruce Springsteen and Brian Fallon singing dingy bar songs about the good old days when they were young. Songs that reference times back in high school. But even in high school, I'm not sure I was happy. I had a lot of shit going on in high school. I was often balancing a big game coming up with which girl may or may not like me and the tests I didn't care about with the scrounging of dollar bills to get a little bit of pot. I was probably a little more strapped than happy. I remember one day, we were having a particularly poor football practice and our coach stopped drills out of disgust and brought us all in for a big talk.

"I know you're tired. I know it's the middle of the week and it's the middle of the season and the weather is shit and none of you want to be here right now. But that's what men do. Men grab their hard hats, go to work, and do what needs to be done."

A little old school and sexist? Yeah, maybe. But he did have a good point. It's not really about being happy. You're never going to be happy because whatever makes you happy now will either be taken away and you'll be sad that it's gone, or it will stay around for so long that you no longer notice it as something that makes you happy. You'll instead become desensitized to it in the same way you do to your house, your car, your clothes, etc. At one time, those things were far-off goals that would bring you happiness. And now they are just things that keep the cycle moving.

Okay, so no happiness. That's kind of a depressing thought, isn't it? The idea that the things that make you happy can only fade or make you unhappy later. The Declaration of Independence even stops short of saying that it is your right to be happy. You only have the right to the pursuit of happiness, whatever that may mean to you. When I consider that, I think of the Greek myth of Sisyphus.

150

Sisyphus was a mortal king who was able to dupe death twice. The gods were so mad at him that when death finally took him, they sentenced him to roll a ball up the side of a mountain, only to get to the top and have to start all over again for all eternity. French philosopher Albert Camus used this myth to illustrate the point that we must imagine Sisyphus happy. We know that the task laid out for him is a hopeless one. He will never finish what he seeks to do. There will always be another mountain to roll this damn ball up. But we must imagine that the task itself is enough to keep Sisyphus happy.

Alan Watts, the philosopher credited with bringing Buddhism to the West, took a similar point of view when he suggested that all of life is just a game, and the point is to keep the game going.

"The angels must keep winning, but never win. The devils must keep losing, but never lose," he said.

Another interesting thought. This basically destroys the Christian idea of heaven because heaven is supposed to be eternal paradise. But knowing what we know about the human mind, it's hard to believe that we could ever live in paradise. The best-case scenario is that we get extremely bored. There's no way that anything could be "perfect" for all eternity. The word perfect only exists as a contradiction to things that are imperfect. Even the *Matrix* suggests that humans could never accept utopia. The first simulation that the machines made for the human crops was meant to be perfect and the brain immediately rejected it. The human mind simply couldn't cope.

Basically, we are doomed. From a strictly philosophical approach and my perspective, you can never achieve happiness. It's something that might show up and tap you on the shoulder once in a while, but for the most part, your attempts to get there will be fruitless. Then why bother?

This is the biggest question that has bugged philosophers since the beginning of history. Is life worth living?

Hard to say. I've certainly had times where I thought the answer was yes. I've definitely had times where I thought the answer was no. This leads us to the question of suicide and whether or not it's okay. One Zen answer to the question I've read is it's not. It's not okay to commit suicide because no matter how disconnected you think you are, your death will still have an effect felt throughout the universe that you cannot separate yourself from. Your family would be heartbroken. Don't have any family? Someone would still find your body and be impacted by that discovery. There's no escaping your connection.

I, for one, disagree. I don't see anything particularly wrong with suicide. I'm still in support of suicide prevention hotlines and things like that to help people think deeply before making a rash decision they cannot take back. I'm also saying that it's your life and it's always your choice. From my time spent working in the Western medical system, I've seen people that have reached old old age and are simply at the point where they cannot die. We've kept them alive and drugged up for so long that there is just no way for them to go. We don't allow them enough movement to actually move their body to potentially fall and die. They don't do enough physical activity to need any sufficient nourishment. They basically wake up in bed, stay in bed, and then go to sleep in bed. Some of the people are mentally cognitive. And if they enjoy their quality of life, then I am all for it. Again, the issue is choice because I think some people hit a point where they are no longer with it enough to make that decision. But if five years earlier had you drawn them a picture of their day-to-day life, I think they would have made the choice to check out. I have a deep nagging fear of being stuck in a hospital bed with no way out until my mind slowly turns to mush and I don't even see it happening. I like to believe that I have the option to ask for the check when I'm ready to be done.

To some extent, I think that can be a really cool way to look at life too. In Tolkien's *Silmarillion*, which encompasses the history of Middle Earth, it is said that the elves were the first children created and they were the favorites, so they were given eternal life. They could only die by steel or a lack of will to live any longer. When men came along, the Valar granted them the gift of death. It was thought that it would give them rest at the end of a life potentially filled with darkness, danger, sadness, and all the other unfavorable things mortals experience. It wasn't until men started to amass great power or wealth that they started to cling to life longer than they should and fear the darkness. There's an old saying that goes, "I'd rather die ten years too early than ten minutes too late." Jim Morrison of The Doors said something to the effect of he only got to die once and he really wanted the experience. He didn't want to miss it in some kind of drunken stupor or overdose.

Why am I always going on about death? I'm honestly not sure. It could be that I was introduced to some of these weird afterlife concepts in early church-going days. Maybe *The Nightmare Before Christmas* really got to me and I want to know if I get to wander around as a skeleton when all is said and done. But the question is a big one. It's really *the* biggest one because one thing that unites all of humanity is death. Seven billion people are on the planet right now. All of them will die. It's an uncomfortable truth, but a truth nonetheless. I like to stare that death right in the face from time to time so that I'm ready for it when it comes. I don't think the Grim Reaper will sneak up on me. I think I'll see him coming from a mile away and see if he wants to join me for one last beer before we hit the road to wherever it is he is going to take me.

Maybe all of this sounds depressing to you. That's fair. It just doesn't seem like that to me. It seems more real than anything, to be honest. I like the thought of recognizing death in every moment because by association, I can recognize life. A bicycle company based out of Phoenix called The Heavy Pedal boasts the slogan "Closer to Death, Closer to God." I've got the hat and I think about the phrase often. The times where we come close to death, whether it's a hike you didn't think you would make it through, a swim that went a little too long, or even a drug dosage that had you seeing the light, we feel most alive. Chances are that when you write your memoir, you'll think back on those moments as a time when you felt most alive. Being alive is literally always happening. You're sitting in your nice comfy chair right now with a warm cup of tea reading the dosed-out ramblings of a wannabe yogi strung out on life and death and the pursuit of unachievable happiness and you don't notice it, but you're alive. You only notice it when it feels like it might be taken away. In the moments when you think you might not make it, you become incredibly aware of the alternative to this whole living experiment.

So my considerations of death are less about being gloomy and foreboding and more about waking up my own sleepy self to the incredible life that is going on around me. Stare out the window on a rainy day and see the glass start to fog up. Sit in the grass and watch the clouds roll by. Go for a walk in your neighborhood with headphones on and turn that walk into a little dance. These are all amazing things because they are happening now, in this moment, and you are here to see it. Isn't that crazy? You're existing at the exact moment in history that this cloud passed overhead. The odds are insurmountable. And when you realize the finality of it all and the hopelessness of it all, it's not really sad. It's liberating. You are free. Free from responsibilities, from obligations, from successes, and from failures. You are free because there is no end game here. Just the game itself. Recognize that, and you open yourself up to all sorts of fun.

Phew. That was a lot. And much more difficult than I expected. But don't worry. I'll be fine. I'm sure I'll get my feet back on the floor momentarily. Just give me a minute…

Chapter 17

BAD TRIPS AND GOOD HANGOVERS

The further I fall into this whole life thing, the more I start to see that everything really just boils down to perspective. The vantage point I view an event from may be terribly skewed when compared to how someone else saw the same exact moment play out. There is no real truth. There are tons of sayings about how the victors are the ones who write the history books, with the losers and disenfranchised crying out that that's not how it really happened. But the victors have their own point of view. It'd all be much simpler if this was *Lord of the Rings*. No men were on the side of Sauron. It was a black and white fact that orcs and goblins were bad. There could be no reasoning with them. King Théoden, weary from battle and about to give up all hope at Helm's deep, asks Aragon, "What can men do against such reckless hate?" Wouldn't our choices be so much simpler if this were the case? If the board was set, the objective was clear, and all of our collective focus could unite into one universal consciousness.

But it's never *gonna* happen.

And let me tell you why that's kind of cool.

Contrary to what the last chapter may have presented, I don't regularly take psychedelic drugs for recreational purposes. But I do dabble. And the great quarantine of 2020 has left a lot of time for, well, dabbling.

In 2019, I spent three weeks following a regimen of micro-dosing. Micro-dosing is a way of taking mushrooms or acid so that you don't go full electric-colored school bus but still feel a little bit wavy in your day-to-day life. There is a ton of research being done by Paul Stamets that suggests this could be a more effective way of treating depression, PTSD, and a host of other neurological ailments. My three weeks went well. I feel like I began to lose my sense of cynicism. It was a bit easier to connect with people on a regular basis. The anxiety of social situations seemed to fade away. Granted, there was a day or two where I messed up some of the dosings and things got weirder than I would have liked, but for the most part, it went off without a hitch and was a positive experience.

So in March of 2020, work stopped, yoga was canceled, and we were told to stay indoors. I had just happened to have moved into a big house just outside of Santa Monica with four roommates. We had a porch and a garage out back that had been turned into a gym with all of the essentials. With nothing to do but wake up and work out, it was the right time to get back into a small regiment. Every day I would wake up, meditate, take care of whatever type of work I had to do to keep my small business afloat, and then make myself a batch of special tea. The doses started very small. I have had bad trips on mushrooms before and it was not a place that I wanted to go back to.

The doses gave me feelings of lightness. I felt a little less anxious about the fact that I had been laid off from all my teaching gigs and had no new clients coming down the funnel for physical therapy. I felt a little more connected to the people I surrounded myself with. There was even one girl with who I had had several poor encounters that kept coming to our house, being a friend of one of my roommates, and even she seemed to soften and make a little more sense to me. So things were going well. I was writing more. I was meditating more. I was feeling into my body. But with drugs, you tend to get a little bit cocky. You take the same dosage you took yesterday and think that you would like to go a little bit deeper. You think that you can handle more and that some universal secrets might be just around the corner.

So on Sunday, I upped the ante. After a particularly intense late morning workout, I went up to my room to prepare my tea. I doubled the dose in the loose leaf tea strainer my mom had sent me and ate some mushrooms straight out of the bag. I also added a little bit of Peppermint Schnapps to the tea concoction, but that had more to do with taste than anything (I highly recommend it for flavor). I brought my poi balls and kaleidoscope goggles to the crew on the porch. Everyone had upped their dosage for this Sunday, leaning more toward trip than just altered feelings of connection.

It started pretty well. It always does. We sat in our regular circle, baking in the sun, sometimes discussing what we thought might happen with the world and the virus. Sometimes failing miserably at different poi tricks. Sometimes just watching the clouds move in the sky.

But then it hit.

It always starts the same way for me. I'll be looking at something relatively normal and it starts to breathe at me a little more like there's an expansion followed by a gentle recoil. The week prior I had been getting that feeling regularly and I would lean into it. I'd tell myself that this was exactly what I wanted when I made the tea. That inner monologue would set me straight into feeling like this was supposed to be happening.

But sometimes that doesn't work. Sometimes the smoker on the side of the porch starts breathing at you, so you stare at it for a little bit and then pick something else to look at. Then the rocking chair starts rocking, but not in the typical way that it would be rocking if someone was sitting in it. And then the patchwork clouds behind your favorite palm tree seem to get much closer to you as the tree itself recedes into the distance. Before you know it, there is nowhere to look that feels normal. That's not an inherently bad thing. Again, you take these mind-altering drugs to skew your senses and unlock your perception. But sometimes you want to have a little bit of a home base where you can breathe regularly for a while. And no matter what I looked at, I could only last a couple of moments before I had to find a different focus point trying to escape this deep, deep discomfort, if only for a second.

At this point, I excused myself. And by excused myself, I mean I said nothing to anyone and walked upstairs to be alone in my room. With drugs, there's a certain sense of paranoia that sometimes comes over me, like I must be the only one who is feeling these things. In reality, the day after this trip I spoke to my roommate who admitted to being on another planet himself. Maybe if I had just verbalized my feelings, we could have connected and I may have felt better. Well, there's always next time.

Instead, I found myself alone in my room, tripping balls, and trying desperately to get my feet on the floor as my brain traveled out into the ether. My go-to recently when things start to seem like a little much is yoga. I got on the floor in my room and just started stretching my body out, trying to see if the bad feeling deep inside me could be unlocked in some stretch or pose. As I rolled out my wrists on the floor, I noticed the patterns on the gray wood flooring were moving a bit too much for my liking. I reached for my mat and placed it underneath me, but the plain black mat I "borrowed" from core power began to pick up the light from my window, making rainbow speckles bounce off the floor and into my eyes. Once again, with everything seeming like a bit much, I gave up on yoga.

Then a thought occurred to me. During this whole quarantine, I had known tons of instructors who jumped on Instagram and began teaching live classes, posting their workouts, and doing challenges. This initially hit me the wrong way, like these people who were supposed to be so deeply spiritual and in touch with their practice just refused to sit with the reality of what was going on and instead tried to run into something that felt comfortable and would make them feel like everything was perfectly fine. I didn't like that. I liked my meditation. I liked sitting still on a cushion and allowing all the shit to bubble up inside of me and being so non-reactive to it that I could bring that into my everyday life.

So I crossed my room from one end to the other, which honestly took a little bit of convincing in my mind. I knew I didn't like the spot I was standing in, but I wasn't entirely sure that the other side of the room would be better. Hell, it could be worse. But sooner or later, you've got to do something, so I tiptoed across the room over to my altar.

I've been working on my altar for years. It has a Buddha, which was my first purchase in Arizona at a Ross store; a troll my sister brought me from Norway, which represents the traveler and journeyman in me; a skeleton in tiger pajamas that my best friend got me in Jerome Arizona, which recognizes the weirdo in me; a leprechaun from my Irish grandmother's house for luck; an amethyst dragon from a past girlfriend's trip to China; two stolen ace of spade cards; and several gems and stones to balance out all of my energy. Above the first Buddha sits a Banksy picture of a broken Buddha in the rain with a bloody nose and neck brace. Above him sits a small piece of artwork featuring a peacefully meditating man's silhouette in the mountains that I got after my first Zen retreat. At the top is a card from one of my patients that depicts some samurais and Japanese lettering that I have no idea the meaning of but still feels helpful.

None of this helped.

I sat down trying to just breathe and sit with the situation that I had placed myself in, but the leprechaun and the troll had these little smirks that suggested they were in cahoots with each other. The dragon seemed more inanimate than he usually was. Both Buddhas seemed disinterested in my peril. But at this point, I was there. I knew I didn't like where I was, but I wasn't really sure of what else I could do to bring myself down to Earth. Hunter Thompson has a line that goes, "Buy the ticket and take the ride." Well, I was on the ride and a quick look at the time on my phone made me realize that this ride was nowhere close to being over.

Debates followed in my head. It was kind of like a political debate where nobody is really offering any solutions, they are just pointing out that the other party is wrong. From the corner of my window, I could see my hammock out on the porch. That felt safe. That felt quiet. And my friends had left the usual spot. Human interaction wasn't really something I thought I could stomach at the moment, but I knew I could curl up and cocoon myself in my hammock. I thought that might be nice.

It took me a while to open the door and step down the stairs. Now that I think about it, it was kind of like Bilbo trying to walk down the tunnel to the Dragon's lair. Just a couple back and forths to get his courage up, then a deep breath, and boom. Down the tunnel, we go.

I went straight to my hammock, curled myself up, and relaxed as I began to rock back and forth gently, staring at the same palm tree and clouds that had triggered me before. Now they felt peaceful. Now I felt at ease. It was a very good idea to go down that way. Everything started to wash away a bit, but if you know anything about mushrooms, then you know that this is not the end of the story. Peaks and valleys, my friends. Peaks and valleys.

I looked at my phone again and knew I was in for at least one more launch. I was hoping this one would be a little less than what I had just experienced, but I knew that was wishful thinking. I enjoyed what little time I had in the hammock all the same. My roommate came back out and sat on the porch. We spoke some. I have no idea what about. The girl who had been hanging out with us since quarantine began came down to my hammock, gave me a big hug, and told me it was nice to have my energy back. I laughed and told her that I just had to go on a solo journey for a minute. She gave me a big dopey high-as-shit smile and said that she knew.

That's another interesting little thing about mushrooms. Anybody who is on them with you has a certain connection. It's like they know what they can do for you and what they can't do for you. They can't take away the bad trip. They can't really even see you through it and, honestly, it would be presumptuous of you to expect them to help you through it. It's your trip. Whatever comes up for you is for you to deal with. But then she came down and gave me a big hug and some empathy and it was like she knew exactly what I was going through.

And as nice of a reprieve that was, the mushrooms started to peak again and I hopped out of that hammock and ran up into my room faster than anybody could even wish me luck.

This time, the feelings came around with that shitty nauseous feeling that accompanies eating mushrooms. Mushrooms come up in drug tests as food poisoning because that's basically what happens. I was sitting at my altar once more, but this time, I had brought my little in-room trash can to my side just in case I had to do a bit of purging. I don't mind purging. I've done Kambo, the frog secretion ritual, several times and it does feel like an incredible release, but I didn't want to pull that trigger too soon because it was not going to help any of the feelings in my body.

I picked up some cards I had laid next to my altar with different *mudras* on them. Mudras are hand positions that you can use to stimulate different things throughout your body. Probably the most well-known mudra is Jnana mudra, where you connect your thumb to your forefinger in a closed circle and extend your other fingers out straight. That's the first card I picked up and, let me tell you, that did not feel good. It's insane to think of it now, but I knew the second I touched my index finger to my thumb that this mudra was not going to work out for me. I shuffled through the cards, not really liking what I was seeing. I settled on *dhyana* mudra, where you create two circles with each hand and lay them in your lap, kind of like you've got two balls just hanging out there, one from each hand. That calmed me down a bit. I was able to breathe. I was able to think. I was able to close my eyes...

And then came the nausea and shortly after came the purge. I grabbed my little trash can and heaved some nasty bile into its center. The smell was awful, but I had been prepared for that with a candle lit beside me. A couple more dry heaves convinced me that there was nothing left in my stomach to be expelled and then I started to calm down again. I looked at the trash can, with the discolored liquid floating around at the bottom, and knew I had to wash it, but there was just no way that was happening right then. So I left it with the candle and switched sides of the room again.

Coloring!

That had to work. When I was in college, my mom used to send me coloring books during finals week. The rationale was that after studying so hard for so long, you needed to do something mindless but easy to feel successful and accomplished. Shooting foul shots in the gym always worked for me, too.

I picked up my whiteboard and started drawing little patterns at the bottom. Nothing too intricate. I'm no artist. Just a little bit of a border that I could fill in with the four different color markers I had. The green marker was making me feel really good. I was leaning into it and going all-in on the green spaces. The purple made me feel uneasy. It wasn't being entirely truthful with me in its color like it was hiding something. The pink was playing mediator between those two colors and the black was the stationary one that held it all together.

I'm not sure how long I colored for, but the bottom of my whiteboard was completely filled in and, once again, I was beginning to feel better. I worried as I got close to completing the pattern because I knew that I would have to choose something else to do after. I spied the trash barrel across the room and figured it was time, so after I finished, I took the can and went downstairs to clean it.

Downstairs, my sink was full of used cups, plates, and bowls. I'm not the cleanest

person you'll ever meet. As I washed out the trash can, I was feeling fairly accomplished. I had colored. I had meditated. I had cleaned up my own puke. And all of this without losing my mind and my fragile grip on reality. I decided to keep the good times rolling and wash all the dishes. And when I say wash, I mean wash. I was getting into all those nooks and crannies. I wasn't rushing through dishes to get to something else. This was the main event. This was my time to shine. Pots got washed. Pans got washed. The teapot that I never wash because I always make the same type of tea got washed! Once I had a full stack of expertly cleaned dishes drying on the rack, I knew that I was past the worst of my trip. I dried my hands, shuffled upstairs, threw on some music, and closed my eyes as I laid down on my bed.

The next day was a Monday, but it didn't really matter because I wasn't working much with the pandemic going on. But Monday still feels like a day to get the week moving in the right direction. I woke up and meditated at my altar. I didn't set a time frame. I just figured I'd sit there as long as it took. I meditated with my eyes open and I could see all the little intricacies of my totems and stones. I spent some time studying each one.

When the time felt right, I made my bows and prostrations and headed downstairs. All my dishes were clean and I brewed up a pot of regular-ass tea for myself and took it out onto the porch. I sat there alone, looking at the same palm tree that had brought about my panic yesterday. He seemed cool now. Super tall, with some good fronds hanging off his top. He swayed gently in the morning breeze. Today, he felt good.

Everything around me seemed a little more meaningful. Not in a way that suggested that the inanimate objects were actually alive, but in a way that you might see a photo of a rocking chair on a porch and get this deep emotional response when you walk by a rocking chair on the porch every day and barely notice it. I felt like I was looking at everything as if it were a piece of artwork rather than just something in my physical space. I had always struggled for the words to describe this feeling to a friend back when I was in college in Boston. We would stay up all night drinking in some area of the city, sleep on a friend's couch, and then have to get up and huff it back home in the morning. I always loved that. It always seemed like everything was alive, or maybe I was just aware of it. My stunted college bro mind described it as the buildings feeling very tall in the morning. I'm still not sure I'm doing it justice with this explanation.

It is interesting how things can change. Nothing is stagnant. A palm tree can be a symbol for rest and relaxation on the beach one second and an intro to a horror movie the next. Or maybe that's only when you do drugs.

And that is actually precisely *why* I do drugs! Don't get me wrong, that trip was not enjoyable. There was some darkness in there that I didn't want to deal with, but being in that inescapable bad feeling makes the regular every day feeling feel so good. A bad trip knocks me off my pedestal of higher enlightened knowledge and shows me that in some ways, I'm still just a scared little dude searching for meaning and comfort the same way everyone else is. And there's nothing wrong with that. We're not trying to be saints here. We're just trying to be human.

So bad trips can actually be pretty good. They let you really sink in and see the brighter side of a hangover.

Chapter 18

THE DANGER OF GETTING STUCK IN YOUR SEVENTH CHAKRA

I recently went back to my pile of unfinished books to read a little number titled "Wake Up" by Jack Kerouac. It's his take on the famous story of the historical Buddha, Siddhartha. Jack has a way with words, so it obviously reads a little bit better than the more common version by Herman Hesse. It's interesting to return to a story where you already know the main plot. I do it all the time with fantasy epics like *Game of Thrones*, *Lord of the Rings,* and *Star Wars*. Sure, we know that Jon Snow goes on to be the hero of Westeros, but how does *Beric Dondarrion*'s side story play into everything else that's happening in the book? Since I already knew the story of how Siddhartha became a Buddha and began the movement that is still alive today, I was really only going back to revisit one of my favorite authors and see if I had missed out on any Easter eggs the first time.

I'm sitting in my room reading quietly in the night. Siddhartha is a prince. He lives in the lap of luxury. His father makes it so that he never has to witness any suffering or death. Yet still, the prince becomes weary and he decides that he cannot live that way anymore. He decides that he must cast off his princely name and depart into the wilderness and stay there until he has discovered the path to salvation. He tells his father that he is leaving and, despite strong protests from his father, the prince is determined to go. He rides off into the wilderness, leaving behind his father, his palace, his wealth, and his name.

And a wife and small child. This motherfucker.

The spiritual path is something that appeals to a lot of people. Who wouldn't want peace of mind or salvation? It's rare that a prophet or missionary ever sells you on struggle. Nope, with religion, it's all sunshine and roses if you just make the choice to cast off doubt and follow some group's interpretation of something that happened hundreds or thousands of years ago. Yoga is no different in that Instagram accounts with thousands or even millions of followers depict hot, flexible yogis in advanced postures on a beach somewhere followed by a long-winded caption about how they were able to break free from the chains of society and live their best life. You can, too! All you have to do is take their regularly scheduled classes and sign up for their yoga retreat where you will deep dive into the wounds that were inflicted in your childhood that you must get over if you are to move forward on the path. This retreat, by the way, will be held in a beautiful tropical location where your room is a stone's throw from the beach and you can start your day with a mimosa to calm the nerves before the first class.

I've come a long way in my distaste for marketing. I'm still not totally on board with it, but if you're going to be self-employed, it is certainly a necessary evil. You have to at least let people know what you are doing if you expect them to pay you to do it. And in the case of a self-employed yoga instructor, it seems that Instagram is the best option. I typically use it to connect with friends from the various stops I've lived in. But if you need it for marketing, it's free and the general population uses the app multiple times per day. During quarantine, even more. So I don't begrudge those yogis who are able to capably use the platform to enhance their outreach and grow their business. I truly don't.

I do question when those yogis start to believe in their own bullshit.

Because that can get dangerous.

Siddhartha was married to Princess Yasodhara, who gave him a son, Rahula. In the versions of the story that I've read, these two important family members seem to be afterthoughts in the prince's decision to cast off the shackles of everyday life. We hear a lot about his wealth, his princely doings, and his harem full of women, but very little is said about his wife and child. This could be a sign of the times. Perhaps Siddhartha really struggled with the notion of leaving his immediate family behind, but the sages who put pen to paper didn't think that people living in a time where women were completely subservient to men could or would understand that great pain, so instead, they focused on the more tangible harem and wealth.

But it still just didn't sit right with me when I read it. Maybe I'm looking for issues as I try to compile all of my thoughts for this chapter. We've discussed before that if you go out looking for problems, you're likely to find them. Maybe I wanted to be triggered by something so I could call out the hypocrisy of this religion as much as the next.

Hard to tell. But damn. Leaving his wife behind with a child to care for? To me that doesn't make you a saint. Hell, that doesn't even make you a good person. To me, that's Eminem's dad. To me, that's somebody who's so concerned with their own spiritual awakening that they can't see the path that is laid out right before them. It's some type of justification of a means to an end.

We've touched on the chakras earlier, but I think it's time to take a closer look at what they mean, or at least what they mean to me. The best version of the chakras ever explained to me came from the children's television show *Avatar: The Last Airbender*. The protagonist, Aang, has to find a way to control his incredible powers, so he goes to see a guru who will help him balance out his chakras. The guru describes the seven chakras as pools of energy. When they are clear, the energy can flow throughout the body without resistance. But life gets messy and we tend to hold onto things, whether they be injuries or trauma. This blocks the pools and does not allow the energy to flow throughout the body in the same way. The two then go on to unblock all of his chakras from top to bottom.

The guru makes an important distinction with Aang, letting him know that once they begin the process, they have to unblock all of the chakras in order for it to work. He can't be solid in one or two chakras while lacking in the others. The energy has to be able to flow throughout his entire body. This is important because energy has to flow both ways. The three lower chakras all deal with the physical world. The first being the root chakra, the next the sacral, and the third the solar plexus. The root is concerned with the ability to be grounded and sustained through food and shelter. The sacral is concerned with the ability to move and reproduce. The solar plexus is concerned with the ego and determination to preserve the self. The bottom half really centers on the physical world. The upper half is the opposite. Starting from the top is the crown chakra at the top of the head, the third eye chakra located just above the eyebrows, and the throat chakra. The crown chakra is concerned with liberation and the infinite possibilities that exist in the universe. It is your connection point to everything. The third eye chakra is concerned with vision and the ability to see the path before you that you must take. It creates a plan for you. The throat chakra is concerned with communication and creativity. It allows you to communicate that vision. These three chakras are more related to abstract thinking than the physical realm. The fourth chakra, located at the heart, is an important place for balancing these different energies.

An issue that I see all too often is a focus on liberation into the seventh chakra without the necessary balanced manifestation into the first or, what I like to call, getting stuck in the seventh chakra. We all know these people. We laughingly refer to them as being a space cadet, out to lunch, or on a different planet. There's nothing wrong with that. We all have a little drummer inside of our heads and if my beat is different than yours, so be it. Different strokes for different folks. The problem begins when we prioritize this spiritual awakening at the expense of what we are doing in the present. How many religious people do you know who have all the answers for your deepest problems, but can't seem to hold a job or get anywhere on time? I can hear them all groaning as they read this.

"It takes a lot of energy to do this kind of work."

"I really have to commit myself fully to someone's healing so afterwards, I need to take time for myself."

"I have to respect my energy before I can help anyone else."

All true. All valid. But why does it keep happening? Why haven't they figured out the proper schedule and grounding techniques to ensure that they are not only taking care of their flock but also taking care of themselves? By now you know that I have an affinity for the contrary and it takes a lot for me to sit with any type of teacher, but damn if this doesn't seem like a whole lot of bullshit to me. What good is liberation at the crown if you don't have your feet on the ground?

Because the crown is an amazing place to live. In the infinity of the crown chakra, anything is possible. You can see the world for all of its wonders and how it could be if everyone could just get up on your level. But it's just a piece of the puzzle.

I know a phenomenal yoga teacher who meditates with his eyes closed. He always catches me meditating with my eyes open before and after class at our local studio. If he walks in and sees my eyes open, he'll do something funny to get my attention and make me smile. Later on, he'll point out how I lost focus because my eyes were open. But that's not how I see it. I was meditating on the beach once, staring out into the surf, when a little kid of maybe three years old passed me. When he saw me sitting there doing nothing, he paused and studied me for a moment. Then he smiled and waved at me. So I smiled and waved back. At that moment, it seemed that the right thing to do was to wave back at a smiling little kid. With my eyes closed, I'd be putting my spiritual focus and path above what the current situation called for. I'm not down with that. I take my spiritual journey seriously, but not at the expense of what should be done at the given moment. If a devout

Hindu vegetarian is stuck on a desert island with a group of people that catch a fish and share it amongst themselves, the proper thing for the vegetarian to do is to eat the fish if he wants to stay alive. If a global pandemic slows the world to a halt, the proper thing to do is not go to church to celebrate Easter or Passover with your congregation, which would further the spread of the virus. If you're meditating and a little kid waves at you, wave back!

All of these seem like common sense moves, but to the spiritually enlightened, to the devout follower, to the one who lives in the seventh chakra, it's actually a rather difficult choice. Do you disregard your focus and intention of the meditation practice for a simple wave? I still say yes. I still think that it's about all the little things.

People who get wrapped up in the big picture and fail to see the choice in front of them are dangerous. Hitler wanted to purify the world and create a super race, so he killed innocent men, women, and children. Christian crusaders wanted to lead native peoples to salvation in the name of Christ the savior, and they killed innocent men, women, and children in the process. This shit isn't that hard. You don't have to be a saint. You don't have to be a prophet. You don't have to create a new religion that finally has the answer to all of life's suffering.

Smile at people.

Help them when you can. Do the right thing.

That's it. Keep it simple.

Back to Siddhartha. He leaves his home, more specifically he leaves his wife and small child, which results in the beginning of a religion that now has millions of followers and several different sects. The sects argue over the validity of Siddhartha's teachings and how best to practice what he preached because their leaders get stuck up in the seventh chakra. They get stuck on the semantics. But it really wasn't all that hard. Sit down for a little while and see how insignificant you are in the grand scheme of things. Realize this and you will realize how little you have to worry and how little you have to stress. Realize this and you can put others before yourself. Realize this and you can do the right thing. And you can do it over and over and over again.

That's more saintly than reciting the four noble truths or the eightfold path.

Therein lies my point. If you picked up this book, my notion is that you maybe don't have the aspirations to be some sort of monk or great saint. If you do, then you probably found a laundry list of issues and inconsistencies in my writing. That's fair. But to the people who realize that there is maybe something a little bit more to life than just eat, work, and sleep yet aren't about to spend a month meditating at the top of a mountain, I think you're one of my people. I've had the same struggles as you do of balancing the physical world with the spiritual. But I think that it can be done.

Let's take a moment to consider Neo of *The Matrix* trilogy. If you don't know the story, the summary is that Neo begins as Charles Anderson, a pretty normal guy who is then identified as "the one" and sucked into a war for the survival of humanity. When he is told that he is in fact "the one," he takes on the great burden of saving the world. The prophecy places the salvation of the human race upon his shoulders. It's an incredible cross to bear and he obviously struggles with the enormity of it. He is unsure of who he is and how he is supposed to bring about the phenomenal changes that are expected of him. The whole thing is just too big.

This doesn't seem far from the early steps of what we will call "enlightenment," for lack of a better term. It's like you've been living your whole life with your eyes closed. To quote Morpheus, "You've been living in a dream world." Then all of the sudden, you wake up to the reality of existence. You can see different colors and you experience different senses. You see with your heart and you feel with your aura. Not only that, you see everyone else around you that is still sleeping. The thought then becomes, how can I help these poor people? How can I save everyone? Like Neo, the task is overwhelming and we are like a deer in headlights, frozen in the moment. At this point, we have two options. We can shake off that weird little enlightenment moment and return back to our regular life, living in the lower chakras, or we can decide to take on the great weight and actually go about saving everyone and everything in the universe instead of turning toward the lower chakra.

But Neo becomes the perfect example of how neither of these choices is helpful or correct. Neo's friends and brothers in arms prioritize his life above all else. After all, he is the chosen one. He is, in fact, more important than all of them.

Until he isn't.

When he gets to meet The Oracle, the one person who can tell him how he should act in his new title, she drops the bomb that he isn't actually the one. In that moment, she does the incredible act of lifting the weight off of his shoulders. Oh, you thought you were the one who had to save the world? Sorry, honey, but you're just some guy.

Once this is realized, Neo is free to act accordingly in the current situation. He no longer prioritizes his life over others or allows others to do the same. Once he returns to the same level of everyone else, he is able to actually do what needs to be done. He is able to do the right thing.

Later on, when he meets with The Oracle again, it is revealed that she told him exactly what he needed to hear. The enormity of his role was holding him back. When we consider the challenge of the bodhisattva to not enter nirvana until all beings are saved, we realize that we can only achieve that enlightenment when we give up all hope of actual enlightenment. It's not about us. It never was.

There's a reason why I'm so interested in the epics. From *The Matrix* to *Lord of the Rings* to *Star Wars* to *Game of Thrones*, they all tend to teach us quite a bit about the hero archetype. And let's be honest, we'd all like to think that we are the hero of our story. Even in a spiritual sense, we'd all rather see ourselves as Ram Dass or somebody who really made a difference rather than just your regular everyday practicing Christian or something of the sort. But when we look at the stories of Neo, Aragon, Luke Skywalker, and Jon Snow, it is specifically their rejection of the hero role that allows them to be some of the greatest heroes we've ever known. Heroes are never really the ones who set out to do great things. They're the ones who do the right thing when it is right in front of them. They do it over and over and over again and the rest of the world takes notice. They are recognized not for their claims, but for their deeds. The Buddha is credited with the following wisdom, "Set your heart on doing good. Do it over and over again and your life will be joy."

On your spiritual path, it's easy to look toward the seventh chakra. It's easy to look forward, up, and away at a utopia you could create or a heaven you could achieve. Until it's not. Until your faith and your belief system are actually tested. That's when you can feel like the smallest person in the world, with your ego open and vulnerable for anyone and everyone to take their shots at. That is the breaking point. If you're so attached to the end result, you could lose your way. You could do unthinkable things that you never thought you were capable of in the name of some ideology that you've committed so much time to.

But I think it's actually idealism that kills us. Terrible things have been committed in history based on philosophical concepts and religious beliefs. It's that crazy notion that we have figured something out, that we know the way, and more important than that, that we can show others the path that they should follow.

We don't know. Nobody does. And when you travel back down from the upper chakras to the lower ones, you find that your perspective is tiny in this world. You couldn't possibly know what's best for anyone else.

What you could know is what is best for you to do in this given situation. The present moment is all you have, but the awesome thing is that it is more than enough. It's little steps every day that get you where you're going. You can have the vision and you can have the passion, but can you have the discipline and determination right now to simply do the right thing. Over and over and over again. If you do, I guarantee that you will get where you're going. Then it won't really matter if people recognize you as the king of seven kingdoms or the savior of the human race. Play your part. It's all you can do.

So study what calls to you. Liberate your mind into the seventh chakra. But make sure you turn that triangle upside down and work back into manifestation of the first chakra. It's not as cool, not as heavenly, but sometimes it feels a little more real.

Chapter 19

FAILING FORWARD

Quite possibly the greatest event in all sports is the NCAA March Madness Tournament. An ever-growing field that used to be 64 college basketball teams (but who knows how many there are now) enters into a one-and-done tournament with one, and only one, winner. One of the things that make this tournament so classic each year is the likelihood of failure. A couple of years back when The University of Gonzaga's team seemed like they might make it to the finals, reporters asked the coach if winning the tournament would finally get the monkey off his back and add a sense of legitimacy to his career. He kind of laughed at the notion that the monkey was even there. Only one team wins this tournament every year, so it's difficult to call your season a failure just because you weren't the last team standing.

At the same time though, that is the reality of the situation. Each time a basketball team steps on the floor, they are there to win the game. Nobody shows up for second place in a competition of two teams. When the whistle sounds to end it, there is one winner and one loser. Plain and simple. To better understand what makes this tournament special, let's look at the contestants. At the time of writing, there are about 350 division one college basketball programs spread out among 32 conferences. There's about fifteen players on each of these teams. Let's estimate that of these fifteen players, five are seniors, which totals 1,750 seniors in their last year of eligibility to play college basketball. Some of those players will wind up playing professionally in the NBA or overseas, but they will certainly never play collegiate basketball again.

In order to get an invite to this tournament, a team has to win their conference tournament, which is, again, a win or go home format. They can also receive a bid for just being a good team. Either way, when teams go into the tournament, they're riding a winning streak from the conference tournament or coming off of a fresh loss from it. So by the math that we used above, of those estimated 1,750 seniors playing in their last collegiate season, five will end their career with a win. That's less than a percent of a chance of success. It's a 99.998% of failure. Every senior begins their final year of eligibility knowing that it is almost definitely going to end in heartbreak. And yet every single one of those kids lace up for it.

That shit is beautiful.

The idea of failure shouldn't scare us. It should excite us. All of us. The reason is simple. Failure will bring out the best in us. Failure will make us take long, hard looks in the mirror and question if we truly gave our best effort. If we truly shined as bright as we could.

In sticking with the basketball metaphor, let's take a look at one of the most dominant teams the NBA has ever seen, the 2000-2001 Los Angeles Lakers. The team was loaded with talent, but people mostly remember the young transcendental talent Kobe Bryant and the unstoppable Shaquille O'Neal. The regular season was a bit of a slog, as I always find it to be in the NBA. With 82 games, I think it's more than common for guys to have off nights or to not show up with full effort. But the NBA playoffs are something different entirely. In the part of the season where every possession matters and the spotlight is put on the most mundane details, the Lakers dominated. They began by sweeping the Portland Trailblazers in a three-game first series and followed it up with a sweep of the Sacramento Kings in four. In the Western Conference Finals, they met the San Antonio Spurs, who had posted the better regular-season record to claim the one seed. The Lakers beat them by 14,

7, 39, and 29 to sweep the series. In the NBA Finals, they met the Allen Iverson-led Philadelphia 76ers and they lost their first game of the playoffs.

The story goes that Kobe Bryant was actually seen to be happy trailing 56-50. It was the first real challenge they were facing in the playoffs. Up until that point, they had simply run through their opponents and now they were finally being challenged. They would have to come together and play their best to win the game.

They went on to lose game one, their only loss of the entire playoffs, before winning four straight and taking home the championship trophy. But I find it incredibly important that Kobe Bryant, someone praised for what we now call "Mamba Mentality," or a desire to win at all costs, was so excited to have a challenge. This guy had enough talent that he could have coasted and been a good NBA player. He wanted to bring out the best in himself and he could only do that by seeking out failure. By seeking out things that could challenge him to his breaking point. And when you are constantly looking for your breaking point, sometimes you find it.

Failure is great. Failure is necessary. Failure is the one thing that might actually make you consider the *fact* that maybe you're not so big or great or important after all.

Success, on the other hand, dulls the senses. It rewards you for the past and when all the bright lights are shining and all the talking heads are telling us how good we are, we forget what actually got us there: the hard work and the basics.

I spoke once with my good friend about why we self-sabotage. For the two of us, it was in reference to relationships and life in general. We had kind of touched on the subject in person, but it stuck with me well after she left. I thought long and hard about why I self-sabotage my work, my love life, and anything else that I supposedly care about. What I came up with was that I was not, in fact, afraid of failure. Very far from it. I was afraid of success and I still am. I was afraid that everything would actually go right and then I would maybe still not be happy. Maybe success would be just being a regular dude. At least if I ducked out before the race was over, or half-assed my attempt like someone who could care less either way, then I would never really know what my best actually was.

I often think about this in terms of soccer. We already touched on the athletic prowess I might have had when I was about twelve (*ah*, the glory days). With football, basketball, and baseball I always reached a level of play where I was no longer the best player on the field. I may have still found a way to contribute to the team, but I was not "the guy." Soccer was different. Soccer had always been my best sport, but I had given it up to try to play football. I had been going to my dad's games since I was a toddler. I played in the parks with my friends and just generally loved the game all around. So in eighth grade, I ditched all my travel teams and decided to be a football player instead. Some coaches told me it was dumb and my dad did, in fact, caution against it, but it was truly what I wanted to do. So, like the great Michael Jordan, I stepped away from the game at the height of my career.

Okay, so maybe not just like MJ. I hadn't conquered the whole soccer world or anything like that, but I also really hadn't stepped on many soccer fields where I couldn't make a significant impact on the game. I wasn't the best player on the field, but I was up there. And because I never really failed at it because I never really hit my edge. There are times when I watch the World Cup and I still wonder.

Once again, I know that I couldn't play in the World Cup. I know that I wouldn't have been a professional soccer player even if I had not made that costly decision to switch sports. But I also recognize how much of a better player I became in the other sports because I had to find my niche. What every twelve-year-old MVP will tell you is that when you make it to high school sports, collegiate sports, or even professional sports, you have to find out where you fit into the game. It's rare that someone's size or God-given gifts will carry them through to being the best of the best. Instead you break down where you struggle, where you are a liability to the team, where you fail. You take that information and you dissect it until you can use it to your advantage. You can find your own place in the game by understanding your own strengths, weaknesses, and positioning.

But it is only the challenge that makes this growth possible.

And what a challenge this all has been! My writing career began with poems in little hidden notebooks. I hadn't been writing for anyone but me. But then I decided to share. On my Instagram account, I shared my weekly study of the *yamas* and the *niyamas*. The *yamas* are social restraints and the *niyamas* are self-disciplines. There are five of each. The *yamas* are *ahimsa* (nonviolence), *satya* (truthfulness), *asteya* (non-stealing), *brahmacharya* (right use of energy), and *aparigraha* (non-greed). The niyamas are *saucha* (purity), *santosha* (contentment), *tapas* (self-discipline), *svadhyaya* (self-study), and *ishvara pranidhana* (surrendering to a Higher Source.)

My idea was to use one per week and then post a meditation time-lapse with a small write-up about what the practice had brought up for me. I honestly didn't think much of it except it is my own little form of practice as a yoga teacher. It gave me something to work on and something to talk about in those awkward beginning of class monologues.

But the writing was a bit challenging. Sharing that part of myself for everyone else to see brought up some shit that maybe I didn't want to see. It showed me some things that maybe my partner and my loved ones didn't want to see. But it was all there, regardless.

And that's when Beth reached out to me. Beth was my first ever yoga teacher in Los Angeles. She had been a fantastic teacher in more ways than she knew. I think she had seen some of the emotion and openness of my posts and she asked me if I wanted to write a monthly article for her website about my meditation and yoga practice.

I'd never shared any piece of writing publicly that was more than a few lines. I hadn't written anything that could be considered an article since college. I had made half-assed attempts at writing short stories or small books before, but they never did much more than stay in forgotten unfinished folders on my laptop. I'd never shown them to anyone. To be honest, I was content with that. I never saw myself as a writer (I still struggle with imposter syndrome) and didn't know what this would really entail. But it was a challenge, and I do my best not to run from those.

The first article was fairly easy. It was a quick piece about being "the one." Just like the last chapter, I made comparisons to Neo from *The Matrix* and how important each and every moment of each and every day as if we were going to live spiritually. It was my own little welcome mat for the articles. It seemed pretty well-received. The friends and family I sent it to said they liked it. But Beth said I could go deeper.

So for my second article, I wrote a piece called "My Own Recent Struggles." It referenced the relationship gone sour that I touched on elsewhere in this book and then it shed light on all of the things I was doing to make myself feel better. How my yoga practice seemed exhausting and unbearable, my shamanic medicines were making me face my innermost demons, and my meditation retreat made me lose my mind and my dinner all in one night. It was, and still is, one of the toughest things I've ever written. Because it was nothing but me on the paper. It might as well have written it in blood.

Something really cool happened after I posted the article. People started reaching out to me. Everyone could relate to what I was feeling and loved to see it on paper. Friends from back home in New York and Boston called to make sure I was doing alright. Yoga teachers from studios long since shut down texted me to meet for coffee and talk. Another healer I met at a festival reached out to me to express how moving and inspiring the story was. Hell, even my ex reached out when she read it.

But the point is, the challenge to go deeper, the challenge to give not just a bit of myself, but all of myself, to the art of writing was an incredibly amazing gift given to me by Beth. I was fine with the writings hidden away in my drawers and the little excerpts posted to the 'gram, but she saw that there might be something more and that the only way that I could get it out of me was to write something that I truly, truly felt.

I still don't think it's the best piece I've ever written. Since then, I think I've cleaned up quite a bit, if I do say so myself. But you've got to be in it to win it. You've got to be focused on making something better than you think you can if you're ever going to actually do it.

And now here I am, putting the finishing touches on a book. A book that, mind you, I am terrified to finish. It's been about a week since I've returned to this chapter for edits and finalization and it's all because I know we're getting closer to a finished product that I have to share with you, whoever you might be. I don't know if what I've shared will resonate with people or be more or less ignored by most and tolerated by those close to me who feel obligated to read it. I think all are realistic endings to this process.

At the beginning montage in the movie *Friday Night Lights*, the coach played by Billy Bob Thornton asks his top-ranked team if they can be perfect. The only thing acceptable with their expectations is a state championship. Fast forward to the end of the movie to his half time speech where he tells his team that being perfect isn't about the scoreboard. Being perfect is about looking your brother in the eye and knowing, without a doubt, that there wasn't a thing that you could've done. There wasn't one more possible thing you could have done to win that game. That's what being perfect is.

So perfection, success, and failure for me are not really wrapped up in what you think of what you've just read. At least I hope they aren't. The Libra within me is still learning this lesson. Perfect means that I put my all into this book. Success means that I dedicated myself to the craft of my writing and expressed the spirituality, thoughts, and beliefs the best way I knew how. There is only one possible way I could consider this time of my life a failure and that's if I get scared and leave it unread in a folder somewhere on this tablet. If it fails to make any sort of impact for me as an author? Then I'll use what I've learned to fail forward.

Chapter 20

DISREGARD MOST OF WHAT YOU JUST READ

Wow.

We really did it. I wrote it. You read it. What a time to be alive.

You're probably thinking we could have ended on the last chapter. I did leave you with a pretty cool closing line. But I just wouldn't feel right if I didn't wrap this all up in my own self-deprecating way.

Noah Levine is a well-known Buddhist author. His books include *Dharma Punx*, *Against the Stream*, *The Heart of the Revolution*, and *Refuge Recovery*. He was trained through the Spirit Rock teaching lineage of Dr. Jack Kornfield and has undoubtedly helped hundreds, if not thousands, of people with his teachings and his work. And then in March of 2018, he was accused of using his power as a teacher over students in a case of sexual misconduct. He was stripped of his lineage and it was publicly stated that he should no longer teach as he had much work to do in his own heart.

I've read *Dharma Punx* and *Heart of the Revolution* and honestly, I wasn't a huge fan. They were well-written and he makes great points, but they felt a little too 'self-helpy' for me. I get that some people need that and that's alright. I'll even say that it's good. He is filling a hole in the market that some people have decided they need. But his words do read a little preachy and the problem with preaching is that it's typically preached from on high. Think of Jesus on top of the hill, your priest up on the pulpit, or that crazy dude on his soapbox screaming that the world is going to end in the middle of Times Square. This suggests that you know something that nobody else knows and that you've got to share it. That you can save them.

And in thirty years, I don't think I've seen anybody save anybody else. You do that shit yourself.

So let's really cherish our last couple of moments together as I lay it all out on the table. I *ain't* no saint. I belong to no lineage. I'm not even sure that I have a religion. The closest thing that I can claim to a teacher is Brad Warner, who I've mentioned earlier, but who I admittedly have had only one private conversation with, three dharma questions asked of, one meditation retreat with, and read all of his books. It hardly qualifies me to expand upon his teachings and I don't presume to do so. I think a lot of his work has struck a chord with me and I hope if he ever comes across this book, he neither thinks I'm a cheap knock-off of him or a wannabe religious kook. But if he does? Well, shit. What can *ya* do? I have no philosophy degree. What I've studied I've basically studied alone without the help of someone else to put it into perspective. I may have misquoted sayings or misinterpreted teachings. I am not celibate and I have had relationships with pupils in what I thought (and still think) was a safe and consensual environment. I'm continuously unsure of my sexuality and the best I can say is that it's an ever-changing thing. I don't know what happens when we die and I'm not even quite sure what's happening right now. I'm just like you. I'm trying to make sense of it all.

But the coolest thing is that it seems to be enough.

I mentioned earlier that I don't really trust teachers. I have at times and I've had great experiences with them, but that trust really has to be earned. The reason I don't trust teachers is because I don't want to bet the house on one specific person. I want to bet on their teachings. So for a guy like Noah Levine to be dragged through the mud and admonished by a community that says he has no right to teach the dharma, I just don't think it's fair. But if you've held yourself up to this squeaky clean standard and then somebody finds some dirt? Well that's a little different.

But even then, you can't say that the lessons taught in his books are worthless because he may or may not have made one or two mistakes along the way. That doesn't make him a bad human. It makes him a human. Which is what I had always thought he was, and everyone else for that matter, to be. Even if he did what they said he did, it doesn't mean that I can't learn from his experiences or perspectives. It's really the teachings that are important. Not the teachers.

The one right of religious passage that I'm somewhat obsessed with is dharma transmission. The story goes that after the Buddha had become enlightened underneath the Bodhi tree, his followers gathered to hear his first sermon. Rather than speaking, the Buddha simply held up a lotus flower and in the audience, Mahakasyapa smiled. In this moment and in this way, the first Buddha transferred his enlightenment to another.

It's a cool idea because it goes back to the truth that language does us a disservice when explaining events. You can never be told the truth, you have to discover the truth. The Tao Te Chang states that the Tao that can be named is not the eternal Tao. Words are essentially useless in describing the vast enormity of life, which is why writing and poetry and literature are all so romantic. They can't possibly explain what they are trying to explain and they try anyway.

If I were to receive my dharma transmission, it would be a certain validation that everything I had studied and learned and meditated on would be worthwhile. That all of these thoughts I unjumbled from my brain and left on paper for you were going somewhere. It would tell me that I had discovered the truth.

And, God, how much I want that.

I want somebody to tell me that I'm doing it right. I want somebody to tell me I'm on the right path and to stay the course. I want somebody to take responsibility for me and show me the way. But, as I said before, nobody saves anybody. You save yourself.

So maybe you're wrapping up this book and you think that I know what I'm talking about. Let me assure you, I don't. But maybe I struck a couple chords and you're thinking that I could help you along your path. That's awesome. I'm so glad to have played a small role in the journey of your life. But I also have no answers for you. There's nothing in these pages that is certain. This is all just my own little cry out into the void, hoping that something may vibrate back with the same level of intensity.

And maybe you read this book and think it's all a bunch of horseshit. Maybe you slogged through it because a friend recommended it to you or you're trying to do me a solid. That's cool too. I don't think I know any more than you do. But even bad teachers can teach good lessons. You just have to be willing to listen.

So do me a favor and disregard most of what you just read. Keep the little gems, if you could find any, and until next time, keep doing the right thing and you'll get where you're going.

CHEAT SHEET

Psst...... Hey, you! Over here. Be honest. You don't want to read all this crap, right? Maybe this book was gifted to you or you're doing the author a favor by being one of ten people to actually read this nonsense. Well, let me save you the trouble. Here are the Cliff Notes for each chapter. Drop these lines if anybody asks you about this book and they'll be none the wiser. You're welcome!

Chapter 1:   This book consists of the ramblings of some random guy. Nobody special.

Chapter 2:   You can learn many things from a good teacher, but be sure to question their teachings, too.

Chapter 3:   Good parents, bad parents. You still have to decide who you want to be.

Chapter 4:   You are connected to everything. Disconnection is an illusion.

Chapter 5:   The struggle to get to a realization is what makes it important.

Chapter 6:   There is no universal truth, only perspective.

Chapter 7:   Keeping things in a state of balance can help a lot.

Chapter 8:   Balance is an act to be performed, not a state that can be reached.

Chapter 9:   I like a lot of Buddhist things, but I'm not a Buddhist.

Chapter 10: It's alright to walk your own path. Don't let other opinions get in the way of that.

Chapter 11: Don't let words define who or what you are. You get to decide that each and every day.

Chapter 12: Don't try to be a saint, just try to be a good person.

Chapter 13: You can create your own luck by how you approach a situation.

Chapter 14: There is so much more to this whole thing than we understand. You can be skeptical and open at the same time.

Chapter 15: You can only have bad teachings if you choose to utilize them incorrectly. Everything is a lesson.

Chapter 16: The mind runs its own course without any effort from you. Sometimes it's best to let it go until it runs out of steam.

Chapter 17: Bad things make good things possible.

Chapter 18: Try not to take yourself too seriously.

Chapter 19: If you only ever do what you already can, you'll never be anything more than what you are right now.

Chapter 20: Take what you liked, and leave all the rest.

fake it till you make it!